Children's Encyclopedia of
HISTORY
First Civilisations to the Fall of Rome

USBORNE ⊛ HAYES

Contents

Consultant Editors:
Dr Warwick Bray, Mark Hassall, Amelie Kuhrt, Institute of Archaeology, London, England.
George Hart, British Museum, London, England.
Dr Alan Johnston, Dept Classical Archaeology, University College, London, England.
Dr Roger Moorey, Dept Antiquities, Ashmolean Museum, Oxford, England.
Margaret Somerville, Visiting Lecturer in Oriental antiquities, British Museum, London, England.
Joanna Strub, School of Oriental and African Studies, London, England.

Anne Millard has a PhD in Egyptology from University College, London, England.
Patricia Vanags is a Research Fellow at Lucy Cavendish College, Cambridge, England.

First published in 1977 by Usborne Publishing Ltd
20 Garrick Street, London WC2E 9BJ, England.
Published in Australia by Rigby Ltd
Adelaide, Sydney, Melbourne, Brisbane, Perth.
© Usborne Publishing Ltd 1977
Printed by Henri Proost & Cie pvba, Turnhout, Belgium.

Published in Canada by Hayes Publishing Ltd.
Burlington, Ontario.

The material in this book is also available as three separate titles: *First Civilisations, Warriors and Seafarers* and *Empires and Barbarians,* in the Children's Picture World History series, published by Usborne Publishing.

Children's Encyclopedia of
HISTORY
First Civilisations to the Fall of Rome

Dr Anne Millard and Patricia Vanags

Illustrated by Joseph McEwan
Designed by Graham Round
Edited by Jenny Tyler

Digging up History

We find out about peoples of the past by looking at the remains of things they left behind them and reading the texts they wrote. Digging up these remains is called archaeology.

The exact position of objects in the ground is very important. Modern archaeologists work with great care and patience, digging their site in sections and recording each find, however small.

Buried cities

A site may be inhabited for thousands of years. New houses are built on the ruins of the old and rubbish piles up. Gradually a mound or "tell" is formed. The oldest things are at the bottom of the tell.

After capture the city was burnt and survivors carried away into slavery.

Iron arrow head of invader

Bronze spear of citizen

Unburied body

1250BC to 1200BC approximately. More and more weapons appeared as the situation with neighbours became desperate. Then the city was captured.

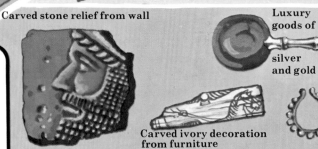

Carved stone relief from wall

Luxury goods of silver and gold

Carved ivory decoration from furniture

1500BC to 1250BC approximately. The town grew into a city. The people traded with foreign lands and became wealthy. They enjoyed a high standard of living, but needed huge defences to protect them from jealous neighbours.

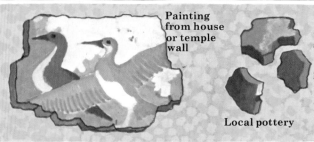

Painting from house or temple wall

Local pottery

2000BC to 1500BC approximately. Nomads arrived and were gradually and peacefully absorbed into the community. Arts, crafts and learning flourished.

Ancient writing

The Rosetta Stone with text in Greek and Ancient Egyptian.

Scholars often spend years working out forgotten languages. This tablet was a lucky find. Its text was written in two languages, one of which was already known.

Town wall of huge stones

Tablet with picture writing

3000BC to 2000BC approximately. The village prospered and and became a town. A defensive wall was built. The inhabitants learnt how to make pottery and use copper and gold. They also began to write.

Copper fish hook

Carved stone statue

Human skull

Mud brick huts

Stamp seal

Fragment of woven cloth

6000BC to 3000BC approximately. Early farmers settled down and built small huts. They had few possessions,

Flint tools

Animal bones

Stone Age people camped here. They left flint tools, their bones and bones of the animals they hunted

Bedrock.

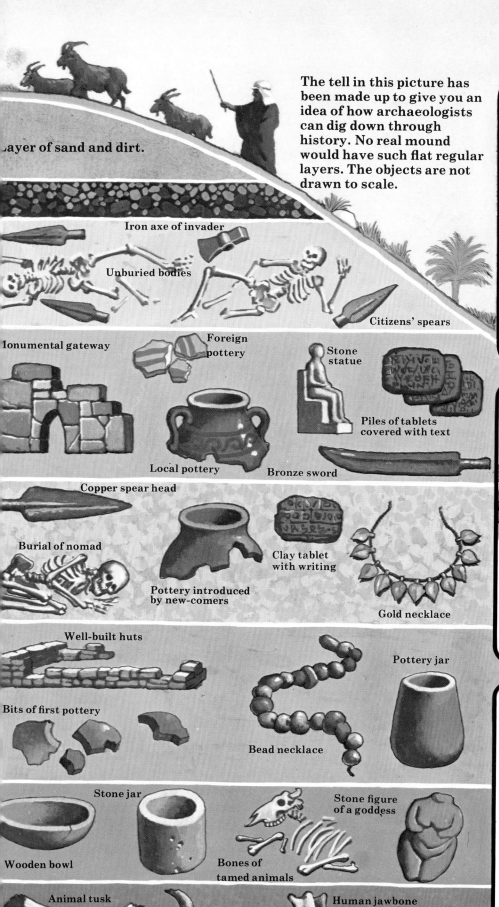

The tell in this picture has been made up to give you an idea of how archaeologists can dig down through history. No real mound would have such flat regular layers. The objects are not drawn to scale.

Layer of sand and dirt.

Iron axe of invader

Unburied bodies

Citizens' spears

Monumental gateway

Foreign pottery

Stone statue

Piles of tablets covered with text

Local pottery

Bronze sword

Copper spear head

Burial of nomad

Pottery introduced by new-comers

Clay tablet with writing

Gold necklace

Well-built huts

Pottery jar

Bits of first pottery

Bead necklace

Stone jar

Stone figure of a goddess

Wooden bowl

Bones of tamed animals

Animal tusk

Human jawbone

Radiocarbon dating

A living plant, such as a tree, absorbs a substance called radioactive carbon, or C14. After death, C14 slowly leaves the plant. By measuring how much C14 is left, scientists can work out when the tree died.

Tree-ring dating

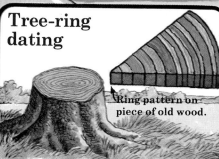

Ring pattern on piece of old wood.

Every year a tree adds a ring round its trunk. Trees in the same area have the same pattern of rings. It is sometimes possible to make a chart of rings which goes back for centuries and use it for dating old wood.

Putting pieces together

Every fragment found on a dig is numbered and recorded. This chair was reconstructed because the position of every piece of gold foil was noted.

The First Settlers

Around 10,000BC, our ancestors gathered plants, hunted and fished for their food. They were nomads, wandering from place to place after the herds they hunted. Sometimes, though, a good supply of game or fish meant they could settle in one place for a while.

Rush basket

Drying skin

Leather skirt

Wolf-tooth necklace

Fishing net

Cleaning animal skin with flint scraper.

Stone tools

Carving an antler

Some Stone Age people made their homes in the caves of northern Europe. They made their tools from stone, wood and bone, and their clothes from animal skins.

The children were told stories of the past by the old people of the tribe. Their fathers hunted and fished and their mothers gathered berries and plants.

1 Learning to farm

Gradually people realized that seeds dropped on the ground grew into plants. They began to plant seeds specially, breaking up the hard ground first to help them grow.

2

By choosing the best seeds, they grew better plants and got a bigger harvest. This food supply was more reliable than hunting, so many people settled down to farm.

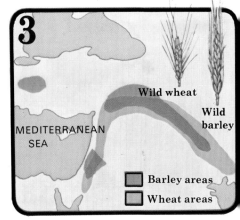

3

Wild wheat

Wild barley

MEDITERRANEAN SEA

Barley areas

Wheat areas

This discovery must have taken place in the Middle East where the ancestors of wheat and barley grew wild. Later, other plants and vegetables were planted.

Taming animals

About the same time as they learnt how to plant crops, people began to tame animals. They tamed sheep and goats first and then cattle, pigs and donkeys. This meant they had a supply of meat, milk, wool and animals for carrying loads.

Building houses

People settled where the land was good for farming. If there were no caves nearby, they had to build homes for themselves from whatever materials were available locally. They built a style of house to suit the climate.

New crafts

Reed basket

Spinning

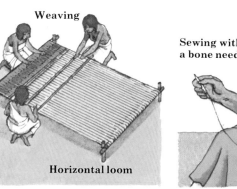

Weaving

Sewing with a bone needle.

Horizontal loom

Staying in one place and farming, gave people more spare time. They improved old skills, like weaving reeds into baskets and mats, and developed new ones like spinning and pottery. This may have been discovered by accident when a clay-lined basket fell into a fire.

With the wool from their tame sheep and goats, people discovered how to spin and weave and make cloth. They also found they could make linen cloth from the fibres of the flax plant. Needles made from bone were used to sew pieces of cloth together to make garments.

Early pottery

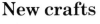

Pot decorated with scratched pattern.

Rough cooking pots were probably made by women, but in settlements which could afford to support them, potters were able to spend all day making good quality pots.

Make a simple loom

Use a piece of card about 20cm × 12cm. Cut little triangles out of the ends to make "teeth". Then wind wool round the card to make the "warp". Weave "weft" wool in and out of the warp. You can join different colours with a knot.

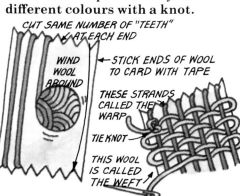

CUT SAME NUMBER OF "TEETH" AT EACH END

WIND WOOL AROUND

← STICK ENDS OF WOOL TO CARD WITH TAPE

THESE STRANDS CALLED THE WARP

TIE KNOT

THIS WOOL IS CALLED THE WEFT

Using metal

Melting the metal.

Pouring molten metal into mould to make axe-head.

Our ancestors had been settled for thousands of years before they discovered how to use metals. Copper, gold and silver were used first. Then bronze was discovered.

Jericho

Near the modern city of Jericho lie the remains of one of the oldest towns in the world. Archaeologists have found some other very old sites in the Middle East, but these are only villages.

TURKEY

• Çatal Hüyük

MEDITERRANEAN SEA

• Jericho

River Nile

RED SEA

SINAI

1 A town grows

Some time after 10,000 BC a group of hunters, attracted by a good supply of food and water, settled on the site which was to become the town of Jericho.

2 *Cut-away wall*

By about 8000 BC, they were living in a village and had probably begun to farm, though they had not learned how to make pottery. They buried their dead under their houses.

3

As they became more wealthy, their village grew into a town. To protect themselves against jealous neighbours, they built a stone wall with towers and a ditch round it.

4

Jericho's wealth must have come from trade. Local goods such as salt and bitumen were traded for obsidian from Turkey, cowrie shells from the Red Sea and turquoise from Sinai.

5 *Cut-away wall*

Grinding corn

Despite the defences, Jericho must have been captured. By about 7000 BC, new people, who built rectangular houses instead of round ones, were living there.

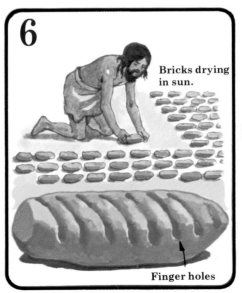

6 Bricks drying in sun.

Finger holes

The houses in Jericho were built of mud bricks. These were moulded by hand and left to dry in the sun. This kind of brick is still used in dry places.

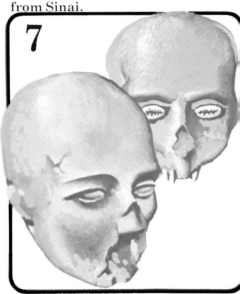

7

Skulls like these, with faces modelled in plaster and shell eyes, were dug up at Jericho. Scholars suggest people made them to show respect for their dead ancestors.

6   *In these pictures, we have removed some of the wall so you can see inside.*

Çatal Hüyük

Of all the ancient settlements found so far, the largest is Çatal Hüyük (pronounced Chatal Hooyuk). Excavations show that it flourished between 6500 BC and 5650 BC.

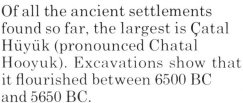

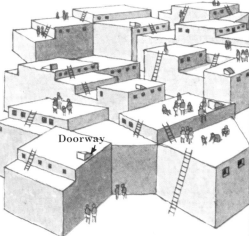

Doorway

The houses were one storey high. People entered them by climbing a ladder and crawling through a hole in the roof. This meant it was difficult for enemies to get in.

Obsidian mirror

Steps to doorway

Obsidian daggers

Carved wooden dish

Stove

Sleeping platform (the dead were buried under here)

The houses had one main room. Benches and sleeping platforms were built in to the walls and woven mats covered the floor. The people of Çatal Hüyük used the obsidian, or volcanic glass, found nearby for making daggers and mirrors and traded them for flint and shells.

Statue of Catal Hüyük goddess.

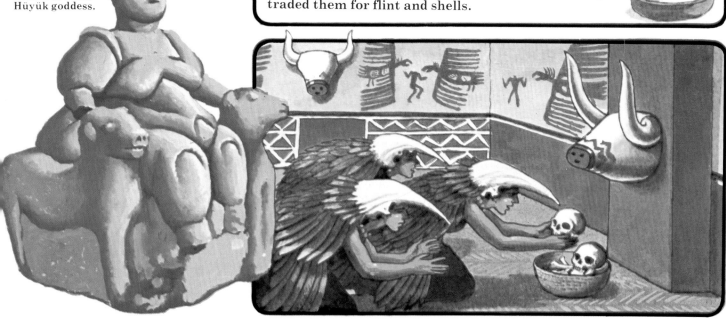

The Çatal Hüyük people worshipped a goddess who is shown as a girl, a mother or an old woman. They also worshipped a god whose sacred animal was a bull.

Many shrines have been found at Çatal Hüyük. Their walls were brightly painted with religious scenes and decorated with plaster bulls' heads with real horns.

Wall paintings suggest that some priestesses dressed as vultures and conducted rituals. Skulls were found in baskets below the bulls' heads.

The First Great Civilisation

Some 7,000 years ago, farmers began to move into the area between the Tigris and Euphrates rivers and settle there. This area was later called "Mesopotamia" by the Ancient Greeks, which means "The land between two rivers". It is roughly where Iraq is now.

Life was hard there. The weather was hot and dry and the rivers flooded, but the land was fertile when properly looked after. Gradually, in the south in the land of Sumer, a great civilisation grew up.

Map of Sumer

The land of Sumer where the Sumerians lived was in the southern part of Mesopotamia. The land near the Persian Gulf was very marshy and difficult to farm, but there were plenty of fish and wild fowl there for the settlers to eat. To the north of Sumer was the land which later became called Akkad.

 City-states

 Marshy land

1 Sumer had no stone or tall trees for building. The first houses there were built with reeds. The Marsh Arabs who live in the area today still build reed houses.

2 The two rivers flooded in early summer. The Sumerians built a system of irrigation canals to water their fields and drain the land.

3 Later, the Sumerians built their houses of sun-dried mud bricks. These mud-brick buildings kept them cool in summer and warm in winter.

4 Every village was under the protection of a god or goddess who lived in a temple built on a platform. The priests of the temple became very powerful and important.

5 The Sumerian villages grew into self-governing city-states which were huge walled cities, with a temple at the centre and farmland all around.

6 Sometimes one city-state conquered another and ruled it for a while, but no one king ever made himself ruler of the whole of Sumer, let alone Mesopotamia.

How we know

An inlaid box was found at Ur. It is called the "Battle Standard", but it may have been part of a musical instrument. It shows scenes of life in peacetime on one side and scenes of war on the other.

From this we learn what Sumerian warriors, weapons and chariots looked like. The Sumerians did not have horses, so the chariots were pulled by donkeys or wild asses called onagers.

We can get some idea of what the Sumerians looked like and what clothes they wore from statues found in their temples. Nobles or priests seem to have shaved their heads.

The ziggurat of Ur

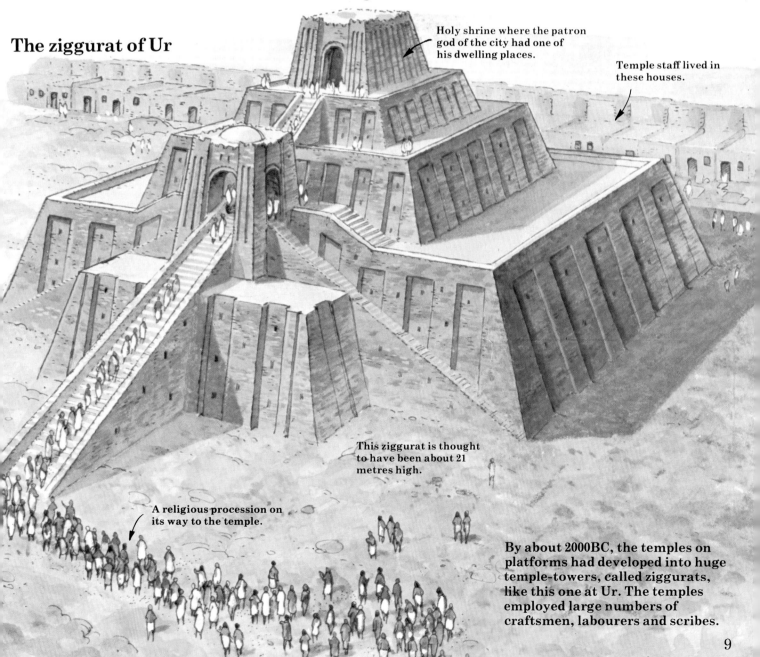

Holy shrine where the patron god of the city had one of his dwelling places.

Temple staff lived in these houses.

This ziggurat is thought to have been about 21 metres high.

A religious procession on its way to the temple.

By about 2000BC, the temples on platforms had developed into huge temple-towers, called ziggurats, like this one at Ur. The temples employed large numbers of craftsmen, labourers and scribes.

The Invention of Writing

1

This stone vase records offerings made to the goddess Inanna at Ur.

The Sumerian temples collected gifts for the gods and goddesses and also handed out goods as payments. As the Sumerians' wealth grew, a simple system of keeping accounts became necessary.

2

Picture sign

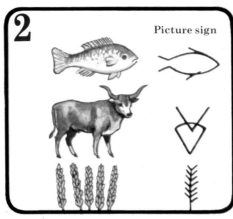

They began to draw sketches of the objects they wished to record using a flattened piece of clay and a reed pen. This is the earliest form of writing.

3

At first, the pictures were drawn underneath each other on the wet clay. The clay was then dried in the sun or baked in a kiln to make it into a hard tablet.

4

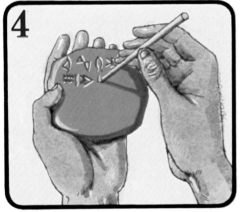

Later, scribes found that it was easier to draw the signs sideways. As time passed, the pictures they drew were less and less like the objects they represented.

5

Picture turned sideways   Cuneiform symbol

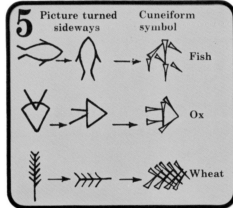

Fish

Ox

Wheat

Because of the shape of the reed pen, the pictures were turned into wedge-shaped symbols. We call this kind of writing cuneiform, which means "wedge-shaped".

6

By adapting the signs and using them together, other words could be built up. This meant they could write sentences expressing ideas as well as list objects.

Sumerian schools

Those who could afford to, sent their sons to school. School began very early and lasted until evening. The boys had to take lunch with them and work very hard.

Assistant master

Apprentice teacher

Headmaster

Boys reciting a lesson.

Bowl containing wet clay for tablets.

Reading, writing and arithmetic were taught in the schools. Discipline was very strict and boys were beaten for not doing their lessons properly.

One Sumerian story tells of a schoolmaster being bribed. A boy got a good report by persuading his father to give the master presents.

A Sumerian market

Sumer had no metal, stone or timber so all these things had to be imported from other countries.

This scribe checks that the right amount of goods is being unloaded.

Writing made the daily business of buying and selling in the markets much easier. If a dispute arose over a deal, the written contract could be checked.

Timber imported from the Middle East.

This trader can keep an account of the amount he is owed for his skins.

Sealing a contract with a cylinder seal.

People who could not write hired public scribes to write letters for them.

Cylinder seals

Carved stone seal

Impression of seal in clay

Instead of signing their names, the Sumerians used cylinder seals, which they rolled across the wet clay. No two seals were alike, so the owner could always be identified.

Your own picture writing

You can make picture signs with a sharp pencil on a flattened piece of plasticine. You could make up a system of picture writing and use it to write messages to your friends.

THIS MESSAGE COULD MEAN "MEET ME BY THE TREE ON THE CORNER OF THE FOOTBALL FIELD AT 3 O'CLOCK AND WE WILL GO FISHING."

Measuring and calculating

Scribes measured the land to see how much tax the farmers had to pay. The fields were divided into equal squares for this and then the number of squares were counted up.

The Sumerians used two counting systems. One was a decimal system, like ours, based on the unit 10. The other, based on units of 60, is still in use today for measuring time.

Daily Life

The Sumerians thought that their city-states were owned by the local gods and goddesses. They divided the land into three parts and farmed one part of it for the gods. This produce was stored and used in times of famine or traded for goods from abroad.

The second part of the land produced food for the priests and temple staff. The third was hired by the citizens to grow food for themselves. They paid their rent with some of the crop.

A nobleman at home

The king ran the city-state on behalf of the gods, with the help of priests, scribes and nobles. Some of these were very rich and enjoyed a good life.

This gaming board comes from one of the royal graves of Ur. The rules are not known, though recently a way of playing it has been worked out.

A rich merchant's house

Bedroom

Servant girl

Master's bedroom

Wash bowl and jug

Ladles and strainers

Kitchen

To lavatory

Servants' room

Water jars

Spinning

Fire for cooking   Reed mat   Grinding flour   Built-in mud bench

Archaeologists found large two storey houses, like this one, at Ur. They were built of mud bricks round open courtyards. They had lavatories and drains, but not baths apparently. Houses like this probably belonged to merchants who were wealthy, but whose status was beneath that of the priests and nobles.

Most ordinary Sumerians lived in small, one storey houses built of sun-dried mud bricks. Windows, when they had them, were small to keep out heat and cold.

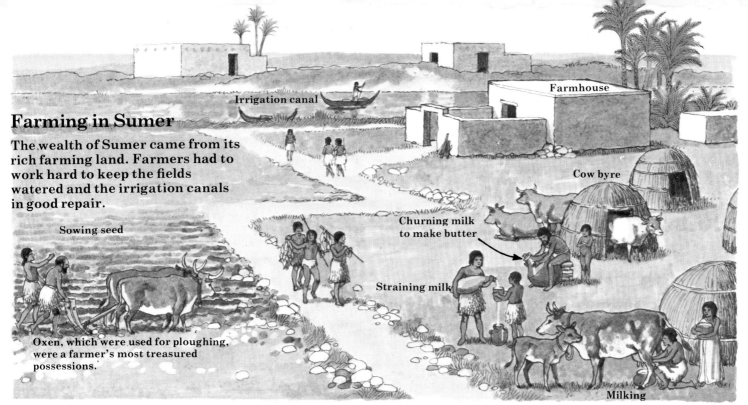

Farming in Sumer

The wealth of Sumer came from its rich farming land. Farmers had to work hard to keep the fields watered and the irrigation canals in good repair.

Irrigation canal

Farmhouse

Cow byre

Churning milk to make butter

Straining milk

Sowing seed

Oxen, which were used for ploughing, were a farmer's most treasured possessions.

Milking

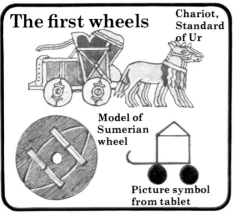

The first wheels

Chariot, Standard of Ur

Model of Sumerian wheel

Picture symbol from tablet

The first evidence for the use of wheels comes from Sumer. Sumerian wheels were made from three pieces of wood, lashed together.

Potters at work

Clay being mixed

Kilns

Pots drying out before baking

Potter's wheel

Though stone and wood were scarce in Sumer, there was plenty of mud and clay which could be used to make pottery. So much pottery was needed that skilled potters worked full time.

Metalwork

Sumerian metalsmiths were skilled workers in gold, silver and copper. The things they made were expensive because all Sumer's metal had to be imported.

The royal graves of Ur

This gold jewellery comes from one of the royal graves of Ur. These graves contain the skeletons of dozens of people who appear to have committed suicide in order to follow the graves' owners to another world.

Key dates

5000	Early farming communities using pottery living in northern Mesopotamia.
4000	Communities established in the south, in Sumer. The Ubaid period.
3300/2800	Rapid development of the civilisation of Sumer.
2750	The Royal Graves of Ur.
2700	**Gilgamesh** reigned at Uruk. 1st Dynasty (line of hereditary rulers) at Ur.
2500	2nd Dynasty at Ur.

Approximate BC dates

First Settlers on the Nile

1 Thousands of years ago, the Sahara was a well-watered plain where wild animals lived. Stone Age people lived there too and hunted the animals.

2 Slowly the climate changed and the Sahara became a desert. People and animals had to search for a water supply. Some of them reached the land we call Egypt.

3 In these times, the valley of the River Nile was a marshy jungle where dangerous animals lived. The new comers camped on the edges of the valley for safety.

4 After a while, the hunters learnt to tame animals rather than hunt and kill them. They domesticated dogs, cattle, sheep, pigs, goats and donkeys.

5 The number of people grew and they were able to clear land near the river and build villages there. They found out how to plant seeds and grew wheat barley and vegetables. They also discovered how to make pottery, spin and weave flax to make linen clothes and use metals like copper and gold to make tools and weapons.

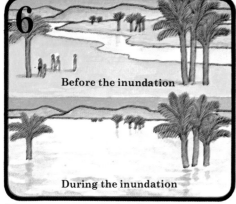

6 Before the inundation

During the inundation

Every year, in July, flood waters from the south burst the Nile's banks and soaked the hard, dry ground. The flood lasted several weeks and was called the inundation.

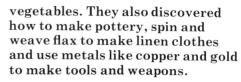

7 The Ancient Egyptians discovered how to save enough of this flood water to last the whole year. They cut canals and ditches which stored the water and carried it to the fields.

Egypt becomes one land

8

The name "Narmer".

The god, Horus, helping Narmer.

Defeated ruler of Lower Egypt.

King Narmer wearing his White Crown.

Beheaded enemies.

King Narmer wearing the Red Crown.

Gradually communities in the Nile Valley joined together. By 3200BC, Egypt had just two kings—one in Lower Egypt and one in Upper Egypt. Then they fought a battle which was won by Upper Egypt.

Here you can see the two sides of King Narmer's palette. The pictures carved on it show Narmer, King of Upper Egypt, defeating the King of Lower Egypt and claiming to be king of the whole land.

9

A new capital was built for the united land at Memphis. As ruler of The Two Lands, the king wore the Double Crown. He also carried the Crook and Flail to show he was shepherd and defender of his people.

Double Crown

Crook and Flail

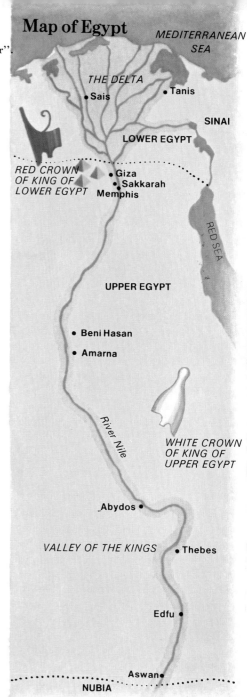

Map of Egypt

MEDITERRANEAN SEA

THE DELTA
• Sais   • Tanis

SINAI

LOWER EGYPT

RED CROWN OF KING OF LOWER EGYPT   • Giza
• Sakkarah
Memphis

RED SEA

UPPER EGYPT

• Beni Hasan
• Amarna

River Nile

WHITE CROWN OF KING OF UPPER EGYPT

Abydos •

VALLEY OF THE KINGS   • Thebes

Edfu •

Aswan •

NUBIA

Egypt is a long, narrow and very fertile country. In the north, the country widens into the area known as the Delta. This map shows the borders between Upper and Lower Egypt before the country was united in about 3120BC.

The king's name

The Egyptians thought it rude to refer directly to the king, so they spoke of "The Great House". The picture signs, or hieroglyphs, for this in Egyptian writing are:

which is pronounced "per-o". The word "pharaoh" which we use for Egyptian kings comes from this.

The Farmers' Year

1 In July, the waters of the Nile began to rise. The land flooded and animals had to be moved to higher ground.

2 By November the water had gone down. The damp earth was broken up with digging sticks, ploughed and sown with seed.

3 Egypt has very little rain. The fields were watered with flood waters which had been stored in canals.

4 The crops grew during the winter. Tax officials measured the crop and decided how much of it the farmer must pay as tax.

5 The crop was harvested in the spring. The farmer's family helped with this.

6 Cattle were used to separate the grain from the stalks. The grain was tossed so the husks would blow away.

7 The grain was stored in the granaries in huge bins called silos. The scribes checked that none of it was stolen.

8 The irrigation canals and ditches then had to be repaired and made ready for the next flood.

9 During the inundation, some farmers worked on the pharaoh's building projects. This was part of the tax they owed him.

Food and Drink

It was the prayer of all Egyptians that, in the Next World, they would have all the good things to eat and drink that they had known in life.

The Nile provided much of their food. They used nets to trap wild ducks, geese and other water birds that lived in the reeds and caught many kinds of fish from the river.

Birds were also raised on farms where they were forcibly fattened for the table, like the stork in this picture. The eggs of these birds were eaten too.

Meat

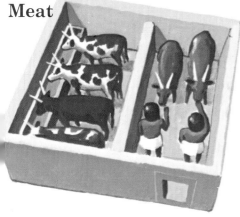

Wine-making

Egypt had little good pasture, so cattle raised for meat were often fattened in stalls. This wooden model of a cow stall came from an Egyptian tomb at Thebes.

Grapes were grown on trellises. To make them into wine, they were put into troughs and the juice trodden out. The treaders clung to ropes to stop them slipping.

Wine jars had inscriptions on them saying where the wine came from and when it was produced. These are often valuable as historical evidence.

Bread

Beer

Wheat and barley were ground into flour between two stones. To make bread dough, the flour was mixed with water.

Flavourings, such as garlic or honey, were added to the dough. Then it was packed into clay pots and baked in a fire.

Some loaves were only lightly baked, then mixed with water and passed through a sieve to make beer.

The beer often needed straining before it was drunk and special pottery strainers were made for the purpose.

Tombs and Life after Death

1 Death of a nobleman

When, despite the efforts of the doctors and the prayers of the priests, an Egyptian noble died, his body had to be embalmed to prevent it from decaying.

Mastaba tombs

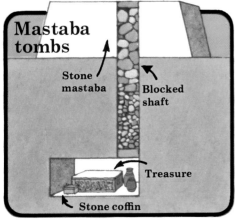

Stone mastaba

Blocked shaft

Treasure

Stone coffin

In the Old Kingdom (2686 to 2181BC), noblemen were buried under great rectangular stone tombs called mastabas. Some contained rooms decorated with scenes of daily life.

Poor people's graves

Oil jar

Box of clothes

Wine jar

Mummy

Poor people were buried in holes in the sand. Loving relatives supplied the best they could afford to make the dead person comfortable in the Next World.

2

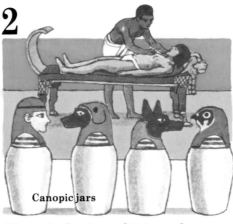

Canopic jars

First, the brain and internal organs were removed and placed in special "canopic" jars. The body was then treated with a substance called natron to help preserve it.

3

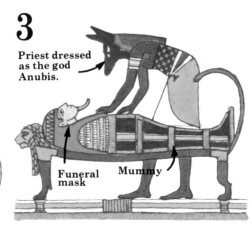

Priest dressed as the god Anubis.

Funeral mask

Mummy

The preserved body was wrapped in many layers of linen bandages, and a funeral mask put over its face. We often call a body embalmed like this a "mummy".

The pyramids

Kings of the Old and Middle Kingdoms of Egypt (2686 to 1633BC) were buried under huge stone pyramids. There are more than 30 pyramids in Egypt, but the most famous are the ones in Giza, shown here, where three kings and their chief queens were buried. Originally these pyramids were encased in gleaming white limestone, but this has now disappeared.

The sphinx, which guards the pyramids of Giza, was one of the forms of the Egyptian sun god. Its face is possibly a likeness of the pharaoh Khafra.

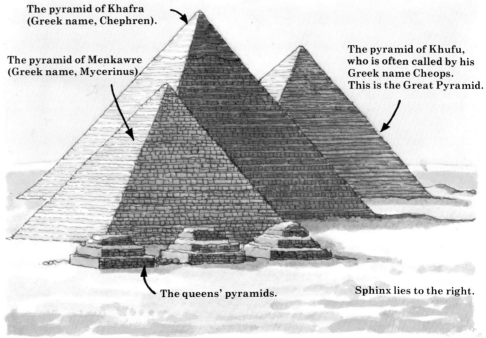

The pyramid of Khafra (Greek name, Chephren).

The pyramid of Menkawre (Greek name, Mycerinus).

The pyramid of Khufu, who is often called by his Greek name Cheops. This is the Great Pyramid.

The queens' pyramids.

Sphinx lies to the right.

4

Embalming took 70 days. After that the funeral could take place. Mourners, priests and grave goods accompanied the coffin across the Nile and to the tomb.

5

Man's widow

The last rites were performed at the tomb door. The "Opening of the Mouth" ceremony gave back to the dead person the power to eat, breathe and move.

6

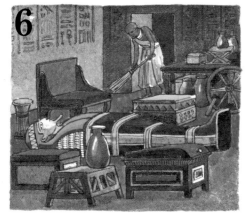

Everything the dead man needed in the Next World was placed in the burial chamber. The priests then left, sweeping away their footprints as they went.

Isis

Osiris, god of the dead.

Thoth, scribe of the gods.

Horus leading dead man.

Dead man's heart

Anubis

The Egyptians believed the souls of the dead were ferried across a river into the Next World. There they had to answer questions about their actions on earth. To help them, the priests wrote the Book of the Dead, which told them what to say and do. In the presence of Osiris, god of the dead, the person's heart was weighed against a feather representing truth. If the scales balanced the person had led a good life and went to eternal joy. If the heart was heavy with sin, a monster gobbled it up.

Building the Pyramids

The pyramids of Giza are one of the wonders of the world They were built without machines. The men who built them were not slaves, but peasant farmers who laboured for the king during the inundation and were paid for their services in food, oil and cloth. They probably hoped that by helping with the king's preparations for death, they would please the gods and be rewarded in the Next World.

Khufu's pyramid

The height of Khufu's pyramid is 148m.

Casing of gleaming white limestone

When Khafra's pyramid is completed it will contain nearly 2,300,000 blocks of stone, like his father's.

Wooden poles are used to lever the blocks into place.

Chief architect

Blocks of stone are dragged on sledges from nearby quarries. Wheels are not used at all.

The blocks weigh an average of 2,300 kg.

Later, Khafra's pyramid will be finished, like his father's, with a layer of high quality white limestone. This will be brought from quarries across the Nile. The blocks will be put on rafts and floated across the river while it is in flood.

20

The year is 2565BC. The pyramid of King Khufu has been completed and his son Khafra is now reigning. Work on Khafra's pyramid has just begun. It will take at least 20 years to complete.

Khufu's queens' pyramids

Workmen's village

Inside the pyramid of Khufu

Burial chamber

Despite their great size, the pyramids contained only a few corridors and a burial chamber. In this lay the king's body in its stone sarcophagus.

Overseer

Ramps of rubble are used to raise the block. These will be removed when the building is finished.

Later tombs

Valley of the Kings on the west bank at Thebes.

Paintings showing scenes from person's life

Sealed passage

Coffin

In the New Kingdom (1567 to 1085BC), the kings were buried in rock-cut tombs in a hidden valley on the west bank at Thebes. Great treasures were buried with them.

The vizier, who is the king's chief minister, comes to inspect the work.

Inside Tutankhamun's tomb.

Tutankhamun was a boy-king who was buried in the smallest tomb in the Valley of the Kings. It alone escaped the tomb robbers and its treasure found intact.

Mask of Tutankhamun

Sport and Leisure

Painted wooden pillars

These children are playing
a kind of tug-of-war.

These men are playing a
board game rather like
draughts.

Lyre

Harp

Young dancing girls

Wrestlers

This is the garden of a rich
Egyptian. Most people who owned
land made themselves shady
gardens to sit in. Singing, music
and dancing were favourite
entertainments. We have no
written music from Ancient Egypt,
but the words of some songs have
survived and also some of the
musical instruments.

Children's games

Child's basket of
toys from a tomb.

Ivory dog

Egyptian tomb paintings, like these, show us some
of the games played by children, but they do not tell
us the rules. They are often shown playing ball
games. The balls they used were made of leather,
stuffed with grain.

If a child died, toys were buried with him, like those
in the basket above. Toys with moving parts were
popular. This ivory hound opens and shuts its mouth
as if to bark when a rod underneath is pressed.

Hunting on the Nile

Tame birds were held up to attract the wild ones.

Egyptian noblemen hunted and fished in the marshes using small boats made of papyrus stems bound together. They speared fish and used throwing sticks to bring down water birds.

Some had hunting cats, which were trained to retrieve the fallen birds. A man often took his family on these expeditions too, and they had a picnic on their boat.

Hippo hunt

One of the most dangerous animals in Egypt was the hippopotamus. To hunt it, several skilled men were needed, armed with harpoons, spears, ropes and nets.

Water tournament

The object of this competition was to knock the crew of the rival boat into the water, one by one, without being toppled in yourself.

Egyptian cosmetics

Both men and women used cosmetics. Oils and perfumes were used on the skin, the lips were painted red, and green and grey kohl was used to outline the eyes. Kohl was made from finely ground minerals mixed with oil.

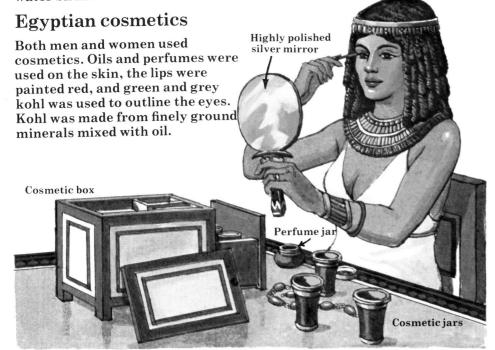

Highly polished silver mirror

Cosmetic box

Perfume jar

Cosmetic jars

Key dates

5000	First traces of farming communities in Egypt.
4000/3500	Farmers prospered, communities grew and united.
3118	Upper and Lower Egypt united by **Menes**, first king of Dynasty I.
2686	**The Old Kingdom**. Beginning of Dynasty III. Step pyramid built.
2613	Dynasty IV. Giza pyramids built.
2180	End of Old Kingdom. Time of civil war and anarchy called First Intermediate Period.
2040	Egypt reunited. **The Middle Kingdom** A period of great prosperity during Dynasties XI to XIII.
1720	The Hyksos invaded. Second Intermediate Period.
1567	Egypt reunited and the Hyksos driven out.

Approximate BC dates

A Great Island Civilisation

The descendants of farmers who settled on the island of Crete were free from invasion for hundreds of years. This meant they could develop a distinctive way of life of their own.

We call the culture of the people of Crete "Minoan" after King Minos who is said to have ruled there. Many Minoan sites have been identified and excavated.

1

Silver hairpin with Linear A signs.

The Minoans sometimes used a system of hieroglyphs, or picture signs, for writing. They also had a script called Linear A which has not yet been deciphered.

2

Besides wheat, barley, vegetables and grapes, the farmers grew large quantities of olives. The olives in this picture were dug up on Crete and are 3,400 years old.

3

This fresco shows a Cretan fisherman with his catch of fresh mackerel. As they lived close to the sea, fish was an important part of the people's diet.

4

Cretan cooking pots of pottery and bronze have been found, though fish were probably grilled on sticks over a fire. Oil from crushed olives was used in Cretan cooking.

Houses

Small pieces of glazed pottery like this one give us an idea of what Minoan town houses looked like. They were probably used as decorations on furniture.

Frescoes

Houses and palaces were decorated with frescoes like these. A fresco is a picture painted on the plaster of a wall while the plaster is still damp.

How to make a fresco

The skill in fresco painting is working quickly and accurately. You cannot correct any mistakes. To make a "fresco", mix some plaster of Paris and pour it into a foil dish. When it is firm, but still damp, paint on it with water paints.

The palace at Knossos

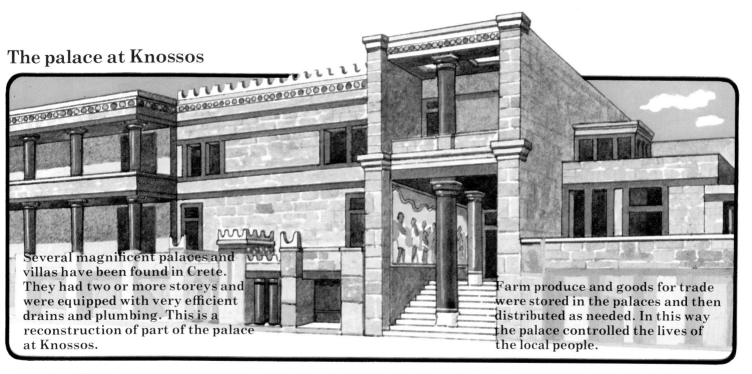

Several magnificent palaces and villas have been found in Crete. They had two or more storeys and were equipped with very efficient drains and plumbing. This is a reconstruction of part of the palace at Knossos.

Farm produce and goods for trade were stored in the palaces and then distributed as needed. In this way the palace controlled the lives of the local people.

The rooms in Minoan palaces were covered with bright frescoes. This is one of the queen's rooms in the palace of Knossos.

These large jars are called pithoi. They once held grain, wine and olive oil in the storage rooms of the palace of Knossos. They were found during excavations in 1900.

This throne, found at Knossos, is the oldest throne in Europe still standing in place. The decorations were probably done by Mycenaeans who occupied the palace for a while.

Life on Crete

Trade

The Cretans made beautiful pottery which is very easy to identify. The progress of Cretan traders is shown by the presence of this pottery on many sites.

According to tradition the Cretans were daring sailors and successful traders. The sailors of the legendary King Minos were said to rule the Mediterranean Sea.

The Egyptians recorded the arrival of Cretan traders in their tombs. They are shown carrying objects similar to those actually found on Minoan sites.

Games and Sports

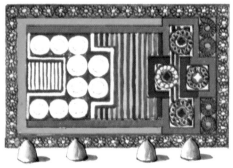

No-one now knows the rules of the game once played on this board. It is known as the royal gaming board. Dice seem to have been a popular Minoan game.

This picture of boys boxing is based on a fresco found on the wall of a buried house on the nearby island of Thera. Note that each boy wears only one glove.

Frescoes and models show that Cretans enjoyed a dangerous sport known as bull-leaping. Highly trained young men and girls somersaulted between the horns of a charging bull. They worked in teams of three. One leaping, one catching and one ready for the next leap. Bull-leaping may have been a way of honouring the gods.

Religion and legend

Although they worshipped some gods, the leading role in Cretan religion was played by goddesses and their priestesses.

Gold and ivory statuette of a popular Cretan goddess.

This picture, which is from a seal impression, shows the goddess who was Queen of the Animals, standing on her mountain. In the background is a building which may be a shrine.

Cretans probably enjoyed dancing for its own sake, but it was also part of their way of worship. One legend tells how the craftsman Daedalus made a special dancing floor for the princess Ariadne.

The Double Axe was a religious symbol. It appears as a decoration in frescoes and on various objects. Actual axes have also been found. This one is made of gold.

Legend says a terrible monster, the Minotaur, lived on Crete. It was half-bull and half-man and it lived in the Labyrinth. The hero Theseus found a way in and killed it.

The fall of Crete

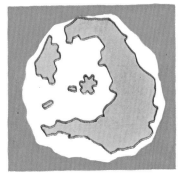

Thera was a small, round island some 70 miles north of Crete. About 1500BC, a gigantic volcanic eruption blew much of the island away. The white area on the map shows the land that sank beneath the sea.

The houses were completely buried under a thick layer of lava and ash, which preserved their walls to an unusual height. Modern excavations are now revealing the houses, their frescoes and other contents.

Some scholars think tidal waves and ash falls caused by the Thera eruption hit Crete and did so much damage that it never recovered. Invaders from Greece, the Mycenaeans, arrived and ruled at Knossos for a while, but the glory of Crete was past.

Key dates

6000/5000	Farmers living in settled communities.
4000	Beginning of metalworking. Evidence of gradually increasing prosperity.
2500/1950	Early Minoan Period. Towns developing.
1950	Middle Minoan Period. First palaces built. Picture writing (hieroglyphs) in use.
1700	Late Minoan Period. Great wealth and art. Palaces expanded.
1500	Eruption on nearby island of Thera. The arrival of the Mycenaeans. Linear B writing in use.
1200	Many sites abandoned.

Approximate BC dates

Cities of Ancient India

As in Mesopotamia and Egypt, people were drawn to the Indus Valley because of the river. The river meant that there was good farming land and a steady supply of fish. Goods could be carried more easily by river than across land.

It was not known until 1921 that a great and ancient civilisation had once existed in the Indus Valley. Much has been learnt about its people since then, but there are still many puzzles to be solved, perhaps by further excavations.

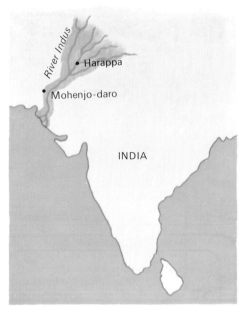

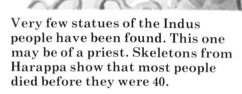

Very few statues of the Indus people have been found. This one may be of a priest. Skeletons from Harappa show that most people died before they were 40.

A street in Mohenjo-daro

Covered drain

Cities like Mohenjo-daro and Harappa were carefully planned with long, straight main streets linked by smaller lanes. Good drains ran down the main streets.

Clay missiles

Mohenjo-daro was protected by brick walls and towers. Piles of large clay missiles were left behind the walls ready for use, perhaps, as ammunition for slings.

Inside an Indus Valley house

The citizens of the Indus Valley cities lived in pleasant mud brick houses, built around courtyards. In a rich man's house, like this one, there was a well.

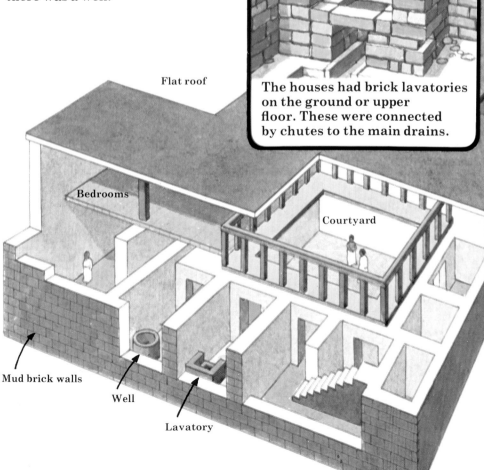

The houses had brick lavatories on the ground or upper floor. These were connected by chutes to the main drains.

Flat roof

Bedrooms

Courtyard

Mud brick walls

Well

Lavatory

Writing

Many seals have been found which show that the Indus people could write, but, as yet, no-one has been able to read the script. They were were probably used to stamp clay seals with the name of the owner.

Make a stamp seal

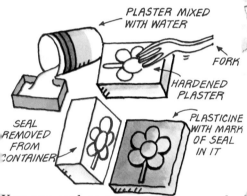

PLASTER MIXED WITH WATER

FORK

HARDENED PLASTER

SEAL REMOVED FROM CONTAINER

PLASTICINE WITH MARK OF SEAL IN IT

You can make your own stamp seal by mixing plaster with water and pouring it into a small container (1). Let it dry, then carve pictures on it with a fork (2). Turn out your seal and use it to make your special mark on a piece of plasticine (3).

Granary at Mohenjo-daro

The granary was one of the most important buildings in the city. Farming was the chief source of wealth. The Indus people grew wheat, barley and vegetables and seem to have been the first people to grow cotton. Several other large buildings, including a great bath, have also been found.

How we know

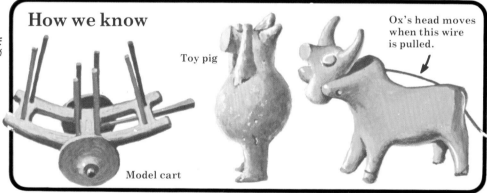

Ox's head moves when this wire is pulled.

Toy pig

Model cart

These models made of baked clay are valuable archaeological evidence. They were probably toys, but they give us a good idea of what kind of carts the Indus people had and what their animals looked like.

Trade

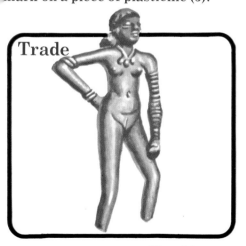

Metal to make statues like this was bought from other countries. We know the Indus people traded in Mesopotamia because their pottery has been found there.

The end of the civilisation

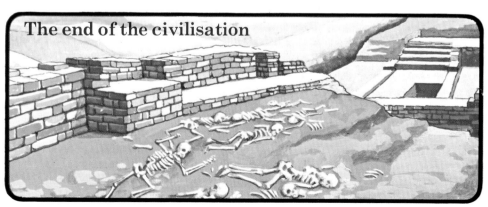

Excavations show that, by about 1700BC, Indus cities were less well-organized and poorer than before. The exact causes of this decline are not yet understood.

At Mohenjo-daro, remains have been found of bodies left unburied in the streets. This suggests the city was destroyed by enemies, possible invading Aryan people.

The Rise of Babylon

1

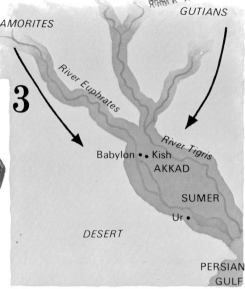

Bronze head of Sargon

About 2370BC, a new ruler appeared in Mesopotamia. His name was Sargon and he spoke a language called Akkadian. He conquered and united the city states of Mesopotamia for the first time.

2

One account of Sargon's life says he was found in a basket, floating on the river. He became cup-bearer to the king of the city of Kish, then overthrew him and took his place.

3

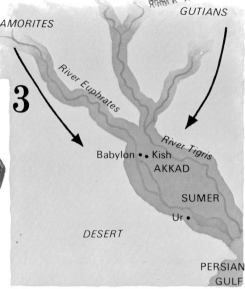

Sargon built a capital city called Akkad, but its site has never been identified. His empire lasted 200 years and was then overthrown.

4

Gutian tribesmen invaded Mesopotamia, but later the rulers of the city of Ur gained control. Amorite invaders, however, were beginning to arrive.

5

Amorite families gained the rule of several cities. Babylon had an Amorite king called Hammurabi, who, in a series of brilliant wars, united Mesopotamia under his rule.

6

This monument shows Hammurabi being handed the symbols of justice by a god. Below is carved the law code he devised. It is the most complete law code known to us.

Hammurabi's laws

Some of Hammurabi's laws may seem harsh to us. For example, if a surgeon performed an operation that caused the death of a patient, his hand was cut off.

Another law said that if an architect built a house which collapsed and killed its owner, the architect was put to death.

Key dates

2371/2316	**Sargon** of Akkad.
2200	End of the Akkadian empire. Arrival of Gutian invaders.
2113	3rd Dynasty of Ur. Time when Ur ruled much of Mesopotamia.
2006	Overthrow of Ur. Cities of Isin and Larsa struggled for supremacy while Amorite invaders moved in.
1900	1st Dynasty of Babylon.
1792/1750	**Hammurabi** of Babylon.
1595	Babylon raided by Hittites From Anatolia, then taken over and ruled by tribesmen called Kassites.

Approximate BC dates

Myths

The people of Mesopotamia had many gods and goddesses. Here we have illustrated some of the stories they wrote about them.

Hammurabi made his god, Marduk, the most powerful god of Mesopotamia.

The priests told how Marduk had saved the world from the sea-monster Tiamat. The victory was celebrated each year at the New Year Festival.

The Mesopotamians thought the world was a flat disk. One story says that Marduk created the world by building a reed raft on the waters and pouring dust on it.

The great flood

Once, the gods were angry with men, and they decided to destroy them in a great flood. They warned one good man, Ut-napishtim, to build a boat.

The flood came and everything was destroyed except Ut-napishtim's boat, which came to rest on a mountain. He sent birds out, but they could find nowhere to settle.

Finally a raven was sent out and it did not return. The earth was beginning to dry out. Ut-napishtim and his family gave thanks to the gods for having been saved.

Gilgamesh

Gilgamesh was king of Uruk. His pride angered the gods and they made a half-beast, half-man called Enkidu to destroy him, but after fighting the two became friends.

They had many adventures but then Enkidu was killed. Afraid of death for the first time, Gilgamesh went to Ut-napishtim who had the secret of eternal life.

The secret was a plant which lived at the bottom of the sea. Gilgamesh dived and picked it, but on his way home it was eaten by a snake as he slept, so he did not live for ever.

These pictures are based on the style used by Sumerians and Babylonians on their cylinder seals.

31

Royal Graves of Anatolia

The people of Anatolia, which is the area now called Turkey, were among the world's first farmers. Later they acquired wealth through trading metal.

Anatolia was divided into several kingdoms, each with its own rulers. Rich royal graves have been found in some cities. They are dated between 2400BC and 2200BC.

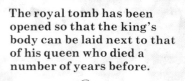

The royal tomb has been opened so that the king's body can be laid next to that of his queen who died a number of years before.

Cattle for slaughter

King

Queen's treasures

Body of queen

Here, the king of Alaca Hüyük is being buried. His favourite dog has been killed so that he can accompany his master on the last journey.

Cattle will be slaughtered and their heads placed on top of the grave when it is closed.

The New Kingdom

The period archaeologists call the New Kingdom of Egypt began about 1567BC. Egypt was already an old civilisation with great achievements, but now a new age began. Great warrior kings like Tuthmosis III, Amenhotep II, Seti I and Ramesses II won a great empire. It was a time of great wealth, mighty temple buildings and religious conflicts. Only one king's tomb escaped being robbed in ancient times—that of Tutankhamun. His treasures give us an idea of the fabulous riches that must once have been in Egypt.

Queen Hatshepsut, who was one of the few women pharaohs of Egypt, inspects her new temple building at Deir el Bahari. With her is her architect Senenmut. The temple still stands today, though much of the paint has worn off.

Senenmut

Hatshepsut

This is part of Abu Simbel, a mighty rock-cut temple in Nubia which was built by Ramesses II.

The Egyptian Empire

By 1500BC, many countries in the Middle East already had long, interesting histories. Then, there was a great new burst of activity. Countries began to increase trade, win empires and set up colonies.

The Egyptians had lived peacefully since about 3120BC. The only province they had conquered in this time was Nubia, their neighbour in the south. Between 1670 and 1567BC, a people called the Hyksos crossed the eastern frontier and conquered Egypt.

The Egyptians built huge forts, like this one, on their frontiers. But the Hyksos had horses and chariots and they galloped past before the Egyptians could stop them.

The Hyksos ruled parts of Egypt for about 100 years before the Egyptians began to attack them. Most Egyptian soldiers still fought on foot, with spears or bows and arrows and no body armour.

The pharaoh's court

The pharaoh and his queen received ambassadors from lands belonging to their empire. These brought riches as gifts and tribute and also goods to trade. Here, Syrians and Nubians pay tribute to the pharaoh.

The Egyptians had their own gold mines and could use the gold to buy things they lacked, such as good timber. They also imported silver, copper, horses, slaves, ivory and exotic African animals and skins.

Lady courtiers

Gold

Syrians

Slave girl

Nubians

Pet baboon for the queen.

Ivory

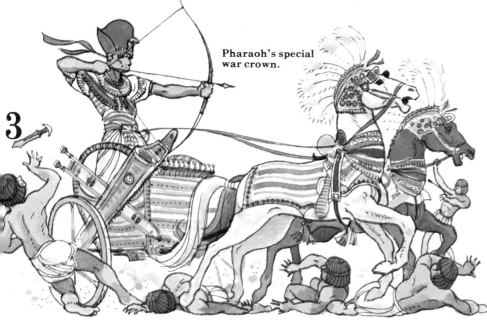

Pharaoh's special war crown.

The Egyptians had to learn to use horses and chariots to force the Hyksos out of Egypt. Then, led by warrior pharaohs (kings), they began to attack neighbouring lands.

Reports of the battles were written on temple walls to honour the pharaohs. Within 70 years, the Egyptians gained control of the largest empire of their time.

This map shows the Egyptian empire in 1450BC. The Mitanni and the Hittites in the north were powerful rivals of the Egyptians.

Trade with other lands

The Cretans, and later the Mycenaeans, traded with the Egyptians. They brought to Egypt the products of Crete, Greece and the Mediterranean islands.

The Egyptians visited a land they called Punt, which historians think may have been in east Africa. They bought incense there.

For centuries, Sinai was the source of Egypt's turquoise and copper. Donkey caravans regularly visited the mining camps to take supplies and bring the turquoise back.

Travel in ancient Egypt

Small boat for ferrying people across river.

Cargo boat taking goods to different parts of Egypt.

Boats travelling south used a sail to help against the flow of the current.

The easiest way to travel in Egypt was by river. Land travel was difficult because of the number of irrigation canals. Here are some of the boats which could be seen on the Nile about 3,000 years ago.

Houses and Furniture

In Egypt, only temples and tombs, which were built to stand for ever, were made of stone. All other buildings were made of sun-dried bricks. Rich people had their houses plastered and painted.

Very few Egyptian cities can be excavated because modern cities are built on top of the old ones. However, models and paintings from tombs show us what ancient Egyptian houses looked like in both town and country.

This is a city street in ancient Egypt. Models show that in cities, where land was scarce, the Egyptians built houses up to five storeys high.

Bedroom

Head-rest

The Egyptians used stone or wooden head-rests on their beds instead of pillows. They kept their clothes in chests and their jewellery and cosmetics in small boxes.

People spent a lot of time on the roofs of their houses because it was cooler there and they could enjoy the evening breeze. Sometimes they slept on the roof too.

Bathroom

Taking a shower

Lavatory

Rich people had bathrooms and lavatories in their houses. The bathroom walls were lined with stone to stop the splashes damaging the mud bricks.

1 Making bricks

The hard, dry earth was broken up with digging sticks and piled into baskets.

2

Water and chopped straw were trodden into the mud, and then the mixture was put into moulds.

3

The bricks were left to dry in the hot sun. It took several days for them to dry hard.

Furniture

The Egyptians buried furniture with the dead for use in the Next World, so archaeologists have been able to find many pieces of actual furniture. The greatest find of all was from the tomb of King Tutankhamun. The rich inlaid furniture shown here is of the type owned by noblemen. Some items are based on Tutankhamun's.

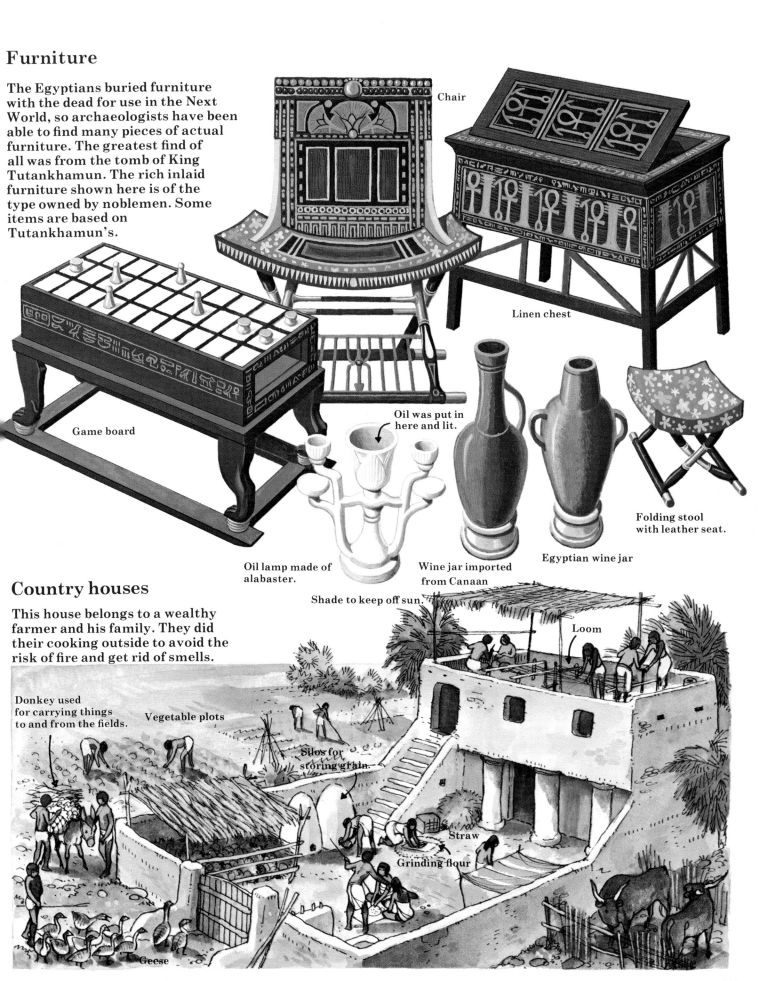

Chair

Linen chest

Game board

Oil was put in here and lit.

Oil lamp made of alabaster.

Wine jar imported from Canaan

Egyptian wine jar

Folding stool with leather seat.

Country houses

This house belongs to a wealthy farmer and his family. They did their cooking outside to avoid the risk of fire and get rid of smells.

Shade to keep off sun.

Loom

Donkey used for carrying things to and from the fields.

Vegetable plots

Silos for storing grain.

Straw

Grinding flour

Geese

Temples

1 The temple

Shrine

God

A statue of a god or goddess was kept in a special shrine in every Egyptian temple. Each day, priests bathed, clothed and "fed" the statue and then prayed to it.

2

Shrine →

The main part of the temple was this huge columned hall. Its walls and pillars were covered with religious pictures and texts. Ordinary people were not allowed

in here or in the inner sanctuary where the shrine was kept. They had to stay outside in the temple courtyard. On festival days, they could see the shrine containing

1 Temple craftsmen

Egyptian temples owned large estates and were very rich. Many carpenters, leatherworkers, potters and other craftsmen were employed in the temple workshops.

2

Reed cut into strips.

Outside cut off

Papyrus reeds were gathered.

Strips soaked

Strips pounded

The Egyptians wrote on papyrus, which was made from papyrus reeds. These were cut into strips, soaked and then laid in two layers. Pounding with a mallet changed the layers into a solid sheet.

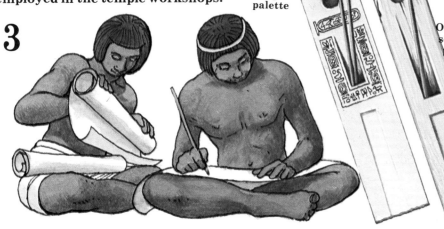

3

Blocks of ink

King's palette

Ordinary scribe's palette

Armies of scribes worked in the temples. Many of them spent their time copying out texts on rolls of papyrus. They wrote in picture signs, which we call hieroglyphs.

The scribes wrote on the papyrus with brushes. Their ink was made in solid blocks and had to be used with water. Brushes and inks were kept in palettes like these.

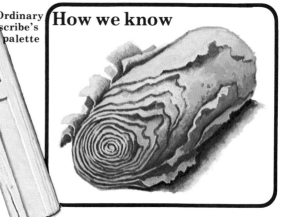

How we know

Only a few papyrus rolls have survived and these are badly damaged. However, scholars are able to learn a great deal from them about life in ancient Egypt.

Model boat

the god. The priests lifted it on to a model boat which you can see here. Then they carried it around the city, accompanied by temple dancers and musicians.

Gods

Osiris
Horus
Thoth
Anubis
Hathor
Isis
Amen-Re
Apis
Ptah
Taweret
Sekhmet

Here are some of the Egyptians' gods and goddesses. They were often painted or carved in the shape of animals, or at least with animals' heads. This was so that they could be easily recognised, even by people who could not read. Amen-Re was the chief of the gods.

Mathematics

The Egyptians were excellent mathematicians. Some of their texts show how they planned buildings and calculated the men and materials needed to build them.

Medicine

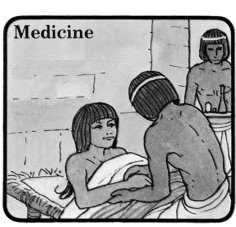

Surviving medical texts show the Egyptians were skilled doctors. These texts give details of treatments, medicines, prayers and spells.

Telling the time

Position of water level shows what time it is.

Water drips out of here.

This water clock was an Egyptian invention for telling the time. The Egyptians also worked out the 365 day calendar by studying the stars and planets.

Make a water clock

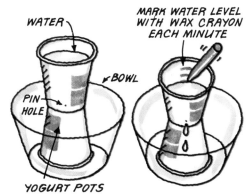

WATER

MARK WATER LEVEL WITH WAX CRAYON EACH MINUTE

BOWL

PIN HOLE

YOGURT POTS

Fill up the top pot with water. Mark the water level with a wax crayon. Using a clock or watch, mark the water level each minute. Fill up the pot to use the clock.

Key dates

1570	**Ahmosis I** drove out the Hyksos. Beginning of empire.
1525/1512	**Tuthmosis I.** Warrior pharaoh who reached the River Euphrates on a raid. First King to have a rock-cut tomb in the Valley of the Kings at Thebes.
1503/1482	**Hatshepsut.** Queen who became pharaoh.
1504/1450	**Tuthmosis III.** Hatsheput's stepson. She kept him from power when he was young, but he later became the greatest of Egypt's warrior pharaohs.
1378/1362	**Akhenaten.** Pharaoh who tried to persuade Egyptians there was only one god. He was married to Nefertiti.
1361/1352	**Tutankhamun.** Boy pharaoh whose magnificent treasure was found by archaeologist Howard Carter in AD 1922.
1304/1237	**Ramesses II**, also called **Ramesses the Great.** Warrior pharaoh who fought the Hittites in the Battle of Kadesh.
1198/1166	**Ramesses III.** The last of Egypt's great warrior pharaohs. He saved Egypt from the Sea Peoples.
1166	After the death of Ramesses III, the power of Egypt slowly declined and the empire was lost.
751/671	Nubians ruled Egypt.
671/664	Assyrians ruled Egypt.
525/404	Persians ruled Egypt.
332	**Alexander the Great** conquered Egypt.

Approximate BC dates

Warriors of Anatolia

The Hittites were a tough warrior people. No-one is certain where they came from, but around 2000BC they arrived in Anatolia, which is in modern Turkey. The people they found there lived in rich cities each ruled by its own king. By 1680BC, the Hittites had defeated them all and ruled the whole land. About 200 years later, the Hittites began conquering the lands around them too, and building up an empire.

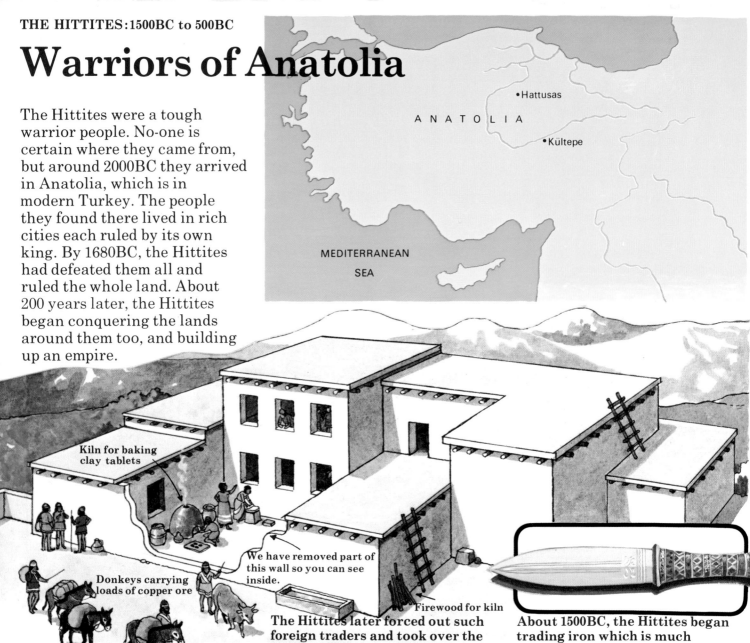

Kiln for baking clay tablets

Donkeys carrying loads of copper ore

We have removed part of this wall so you can see inside.

Firewood for kiln

Copper was found in Anatolia. Assyrian copper merchants built this trading post there about 2000BC.

The Hittites later forced out such foreign traders and took over the metal trade themselves. This made them very powerful because everyone needed metal for tools and weapons.

About 1500BC, the Hittites began trading iron which is much stronger than copper. This dagger, which belonged to Tutankhamun, has an iron blade which was probably a gift from the Hittites.

Key dates

2000	Hittites arrive in Anatolia.
1680/1650	**King Labarnas I** united the land.
1460	Beginning of Hittite empire.
1380/1340	**King Shuppiluliuma** extended empire into Syria and broke power of Mitanni.
1300	Battle of Kadesh against Ramesses II of Egypt.
1283	Peace treaty with Ramesses II.
1270	Hittite princess married Ramesses II.
1190	Hittites defeated by Sea Peoples. End of kingdom in Anatolia. Small states survive in Syria.
700	These states disappear in Assyrian empire.

Approximate BC dates

1 Hittite gods

Carvings are here.

This rocky gorge was very sacred to the Hittites. They carved pictures of their gods and goddesses into the rock-face there. In front are the ruins of a temple.

2

Teshub

This picture shows some of the gods and goddesses which are carved in the sacred gorge. The chief god was Teshub, who was thought to control the weather.

40

Hittite cities

The Hittites built massive defences with huge blocks of stone to guard their cities and palaces. This is part of the wall which surrounded their capital city, Hattusas.

Gateway to city

Hittite warriors

Secret passage

The Hittites dug narrow tunnels under their city walls. During a siege, they could dash out and surprise the enemy.

The Hittites' horses were too small to carry riders far. The warriors rode into battle in small chariots pulled by two or more horses.

Hittite warriors destroyed the Mitanni people and took their land. They also captured part of the Egyptians' empire.

Peace treaty

After years of war, the Hittites made peace with the Egyptians, and in 1270BC a Hittite princess married the Egyptian king Ramesses II. They also signed a treaty—the first international treaty for which we have the terms.

1 The end of the Hittites

Invading Sea Peoples

About 1200BC, the Hittite empire was wiped out by new invaders called the Sea Peoples, who probably came from the Mediterranean islands. They brought their familes with them to look for new homes.

2

Some Hittite refugees escaped to the south and settled in what is now Syria. They managed to survive there until the area was conquered by the Assyrians.

41

Mysterious People from Greece

The Mycenaeans are named after the city of Mycenae in Greece where their remains were first discovered in AD1876. Historians disagree about who they were, but some think they were new-comers to the area, related to the people who began arriving all over the Middle East around 2000BC.

This is the gold funeral mask of one of the first kings of Mycenae. It was once thought to be a portrait of Agamemnon, who led a famous war against Troy, but it is now known to be much earlier.

Mycenae was found by a German archaeologist called Schliemann. One of his greatest discoveries was this circle of royal graves dated between 1600 and 1500BC, early in Mycenaean history.

Tombs of the warrior kings

After 1500BC, the warrior kings of Mycenae and the other city-states in Greece were buried in tombs like this, called tholos tombs.

We have removed part of the mound of earth so you can see inside.

Doorway

The king's body, with his weapons and treasures, was placed in this bee-hive-shaped stone vault. The treasure was stolen from this tomb in ancient times and it was found empty.

This one, found at Mycenae, was called the Treasury of Atreus, because it was thought at first that it belonged to Agamemnon's father, Atreus.

The Mycenaean warrior kings became very rich and powerful and eventually rivalled the Cretans. When Crete was destroyed, they took control of the seas.

Key dates

2200/2000	New people arrived in Greece.
1600/1500	Grave circles at Mycenae. Mycenaeans influenced by Crete.
1450	Mycenaeans appear to have taken over Knossos in Crete. Linear B tablets in Crete as well as in Greece.
1400	Mycenaeans were great sea power. They traded widely.
1200	Siege of Troy. Slow decline of Mycenaean power.
1100/800	Dark Age in Greece.
Approximate BC dates	

3

These are some of the objects found in the royal graves. Some of them, especially the bull's head, show that the Mycenaeans were influenced by the Cretans.

4

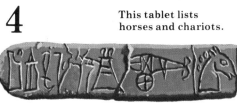

This tablet lists horses and chariots.

The Mycenaeans' language was an early form of Greek, and it was written in a script we call Linear B. Many tablets have been found but they are only lists of stored goods, showing that the wheat, barley, wine and olive oil produced by the local farmers were stored in the palace. They tell us nothing of the Mycenaeans' history or their thoughts.

5

This Mycenaean gold ring shows a goddess attended by her priestesses. As in Crete, goddesses and priestesses were very powerful, though tablets name some gods, too.

Mycenaean treasure

A balloon full of air is tied to the ingot to lift it to the surface.

"Ox-hide" ingot

Underwater archaeologists have rescued cargo from the wrecks of Mycenaean ships. The Mycenaeans sailed great distances to trade metals and other goods. They carried copper ingots shaped like stretched-out ox hides, like the one shown here.

How we know

The Mycenaeans traded valuable objects made by their craftsmen for things they needed from abroad. The presence of their special style of pottery, silver and gold work in other countries shows how far they travelled.

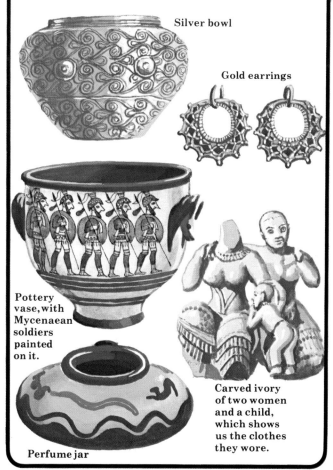

Silver bowl

Gold earrings

Pottery vase, with Mycenaean soldiers painted on it.

Carved ivory of two women and a child, which shows us the clothes they wore.

Perfume jar

Palaces and Soldiers

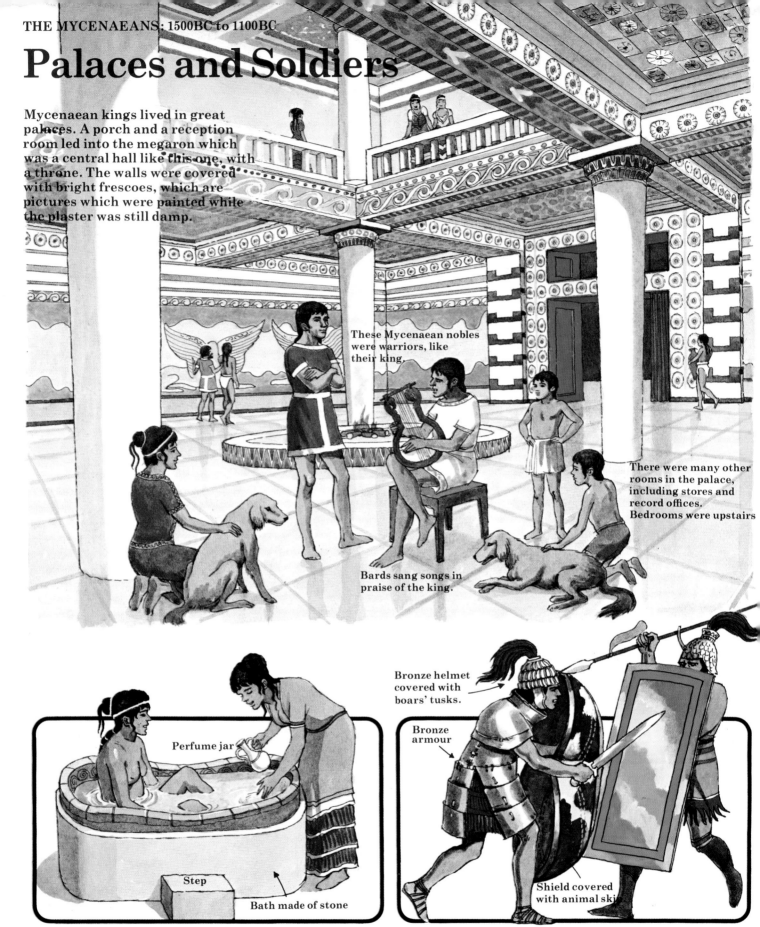

Mycenaean kings lived in great palaces. A porch and a reception room led into the megaron which was a central hall like this one, with a throne. The walls were covered with bright frescoes, which are pictures which were painted while the plaster was still damp.

These Mycenaean nobles were warriors, like their king.

There were many other rooms in the palace, including stores and record offices. Bedrooms were upstairs.

Bards sang songs in praise of the king.

Perfume jar

Step

Bath made of stone

Bronze helmet covered with boars' tusks.

Bronze armour

Shield covered with animal ski

A bath like this was found in the palace at Pylos. Walled cities like Pylos, Mycenae and Athens had secret passages to underground springs, so they had water even during a siege.

We know a good deal about the armour and weapons of the Mycenaeans because weapons were found in their graves and pictures of soldiers have survived. It was probably only very noble or successful warriors who had complete suits of armour and boars' tusk helmets.

Hunting wild boars

Important warriors owned horses and chariots. When they were not at war they used them for hunting. The helmets they wore in battle were often decorated with tusks of wild boars killed in the hunt.

The Lion Gate

Many palaces and cities were protected by massive stone walls. This is the Lion Gate in the wall round Mycenae as it stands today.

The Trojan wars

The engraving on this piece of silver shows the siege of a city. A famous Greek story tells how the Mycenaeans sailed east to the city of Troy and laid siege to it for ten years.

Wars between the Mycenaean kingdoms may have weakened them, because about 1100BC new people called the Dorians invaded some areas of Greece. The power of the Mycenaeans declined, though their glory lived on in the poems of the Greek poet Homer.

Rich Mycenaean ladies wore dresses like this. Helen of Troy, a beautiful lady who was supposed to have been the cause of the wars with Troy, would have dressed like this too.

Canaanites and Philistines

The people who settled at the the eastern end of the Mediterranean about 2000BC are called the Canaanites. Their land was rich and it also formed an important link between Asia and Africa. Rival empire builders such as the Egyptians, Mitanni and Hittites constantly fought over it.

By 1500BC there were many walled city-states in Canaan. They were heavily defended and each had its own royal family and palace. This statue is of one of the Canaanite princes.

This piece of ivory shows a Canaanite prince being welcomed home after a battle. The princes were always fighting each other instead of working together to keep out invaders.

Huge cedar trees grew in part of Canaan. The people of Egypt and Mesopotamia wanted these because they had no good wood of their own. This made them anxious to gain control of the area.

The port of Byblos

Canaanite craftsmen were very skilled. They made beautiful objects from gold and ivory which were sold to other countries. Here, a Canaanite merchant is preparing to set out from the great port of Byblos about 1450BC. He is going to take slaves, wood, wine, gold and ivory to his best customers, the Egyptians.

Canaanite gods

Canaanite
script

Clay tablets, like this, were found in the remains of the city of Ugarit. They are covered with Canaanite writing which tells of the adventures of gods and goddesses.

Two of the gods are shown here. The Canaanites believed their gods controlled the weather and made the crops grow. They worshipped them in "High Places" which had tall stones inside.

The Sea Peoples invade

About 1190BC, the Sea Peoples invaded the eastern Mediterranean, killing and destroying as they went. Here they are fighting the Egyptians, who finally defeated them.

One tribe of Sea Peoples, the Peleset, retreated to the south of Canaan and settled there. This

land was named Palestine after them and in the Bible they are called Philistines.

Egyptians

Philistines

The Philistines took control of the local iron trade. Iron weapons are much stronger than copper and bronze, so the Philistines were powerful and feared.

Nomads in the Desert

1

2

Even in our earliest records there are references to tribes who wandered along the edges of the Syrian and Arabian deserts with their sheep. Such people are called nomads.

This is part of an Egyptian tomb painting of about 1900BC. It shows the arrival of nomad traders who have brought eye-paint to sell in Egypt. They carry their trade goods and all their belongings on the backs of donkeys. Other tribes owned sheep and goats which they took into the Delta of Egypt to eat the grass.

3

4

In some places nomads were able to settle among the farmers, but if too many arrived the locals drove them away.

This statue is of a king whose tribe had invaded and become the rulers of the city of Mari in Mesopotamia. He lived about 2000BC.

Solomon's temple

This temple was built in Jerusalem by the Israelite king, Solomon. Solomon and his father, David, were friendly with the Phoenician king, Hiram, of Tyre. Hiram sent skilled Phoenician craftsmen to Jerusalem to help design and build the temple. It is very similar in plan to earlier temples built by the Canaanites.

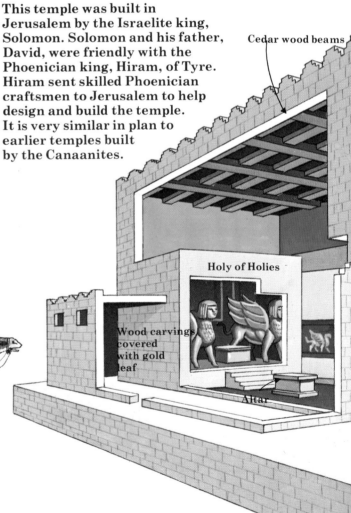

Cedar wood beams

Holy of Holies

Wood carvings covered with gold leaf

Altar

5

6

Some nomads, like this girl musician, hired themselves out as servants. Others became paid soldiers or labourers.

By about 1000BC, people had learnt to tame camels. This meant they could cross the desert.

The Israelites

Among the wandering tribes were the ancestors of the Israelites. After many battles they took some land from the Canaanites and settled down.

The Philistines were serious rivals. The Israelites chose Saul as king to lead them against the Philistines, but the hero of the war is said to have been a boy called David.

David became king in about 1010BC and made Jerusalem his capital. This great bronze bowl stood outside the temple built there by his son Solomon.

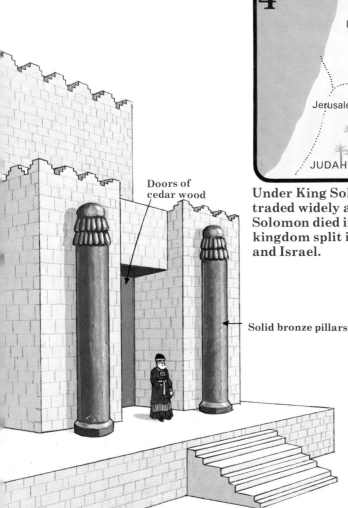

Doors of cedar wood

Solid bronze pillars

Under King Solomon, the Israelites traded widely and grew rich. After Solomon died in 925BC, the kingdom split in two—Judah and Israel.

Gradually the Assyrians extended their empire towards Israel. This monument shows King Jehu of Israel paying tribute to them. Later, Israel rebelled and its people were taken away, never to return.

The people of Judah escaped the Assyrians, but were conquered and taken into captivity by the Babylonians in 587BC. Jerusalem and the temple were destroyed.

Many of these people and places are mentioned in the Old Testament.

The Phoenicians

1 Phoenician city

Phoenician merchant ships

About 1100BC, trade in the Mediterranean was dominated by rich Canaanite merchants who lived on the coast. The Greeks gave them the name Phoenicians. Phoenician cities had splendid harbours and strong defences. The greatest of them were Tyre and Sidon.

2 Murex shell

Glass beads

Among the things the Phoenicians made and traded were brightly coloured glass vases and beads. Their most famous product was an expensive dye made from murex shells, which dyed cloth a range of beautiful colours from pink to deep purple.

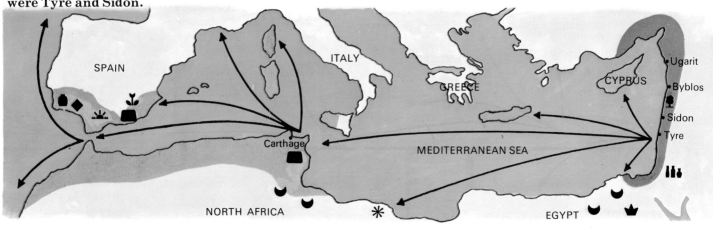

SPAIN

ITALY

GREECE

Carthage

MEDITERRANEAN SEA

CYPRUS

Ugarit

Byblos

Sidon

Tyre

NORTH AFRICA

EGYPT

◧ Phoenicia	☾ ivory	◼ lead	❀ wood
	☼ silver	olive oil	❦ grain
◻ Phoenician colonies	♔ gold	✳ salt	♆ glass
	◆ copper		

This map shows where the Phoenicians travelled and traded. Besides trading they also set up many colonies in foreign lands. The most important of these was Carthage in north Africa. Eventually these activities brought them into conflict with the Greeks and later the Romans.

Carthage

The founder of Carthage was the Phoenician princess Dido. When she landed on the coast of north Africa, she asked the local ruler for land on which to build a city.

He said she could have as much land as an ox-hide would cover. Dido had the hide cut into very thin strips so she could mark off a large area of land.

Occasionally in times of great trouble, the Phoenicians sacrificed children to their gods. The burnt remains were placed in pottery urns, like these, and buried.

The Phoenicians were on good terms with their Israelite neighbours. Ahab, king of Israel, married Jezebel, princess of Tyre, and Phoenician craftsmen helped build Solomon's temple.

The Phoenicians were skilled sailors and daring explorers. One expedition visited the west coast of Africa and another sailed right round it.

Part of the Phoenician alphabet.

Letters in our alphabet which have come from the Phoenician ones.

Perhaps the greatest of all the Phoenicians' achievements was the invention of their alphabet, which is the basis of the alphabet we use today.

War ships

The Phoenicians were famous for their war ships. This one is a bireme, which means it has two banks of oars.

Key dates

1100	Rise to power of Phoenicians.
970/936	**Hiram the Great**, king of Tyre.
876	Tyre paid tribute to Assyria.
875	**Jezebel** married Ahab of Israel.
814	**Dido** founded Carthage.
600	Phoenicians sailed round Africa.
574	Tyre defeated by Babylon.
539	Phoenicia became part of Persian empire with fall of Babylon.
	Approximate BC dates

Ram for making holes in enemy ships.

Later, Phoenicia became part of the Persian empire. The Persians used Phoenician war ships to fight great sea battles against the Greeks.

Life in the Assyrian Empire

In early times, Assyria was a
small, unimportant state in
northern Mesopotamia. For
centuries it was ruled by
more powerful states, such as
Akkad and Babylon. When these
collapsed, the Assyrians had
the chance to become
independent and win an
empire of their own.

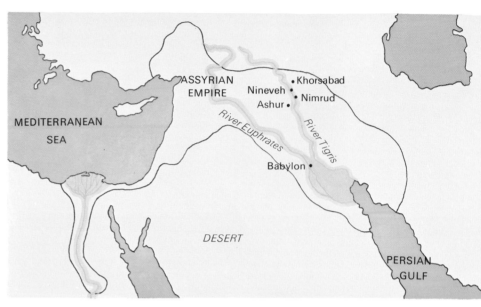

1

This carving shows one of the
Assyrians' many gods. Their chief
god was Ashur. They also
worshipped a great mother
goddess, Ishtar, and believed in
demons and spirits.

This is the capital city of Assyria,
which was named Ashur after the
god. It was built on the River Tigris
so that trading ships could
unload there.

Ashur had a powerful Council of
Elders. It was often in conflict
with the king and many kings
tried to reduce its power.

The Assyrians, like the
Babylonians, had a code of laws.
People who broke them were
punished savagely. Some were
flogged or had their ears cut off.

This is an Assyrian library. The
language and literature inherited
from Sumer and Babylon were
stored on clay tablets.

The Assyrians dug deep wells inside
their cities. If the city were
besieged, the people would still
have water.

The empire

1

For centuries, the Assyrian peasants had to fight for survival. They became good, tough warriors.

2

This is Ashurnasirpal II. His grandfather, Adadnirari II, had made Assyria independent. He made it into an empire.

3

By 670BC the empire was too big to be controlled properly. First Egypt, then Babylon, broke away.

4

By 609BC the empire was destroyed. Its ruins lay forgotten in the desert until they were discovered in the 1840s.

Watering the land

This is a shaduf. The Assyrians used shadufs to lift river water into canals dug specially to take it to the fields.

Stone weight

When the land was watered properly, it was fertile. The Assyrians grew wheat, barley, grapes, fruit trees and vegetables.

This aqueduct was built to take water to Nineveh so that King Sennacherib could have gardens and orchards planted there.

How to make a model shaduf

Use this model shaduf to lift water from a bowl into another.

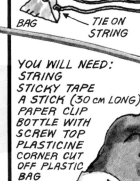

1 BAG — TIE ON STRING

2

3 SCISSORS / TAPE / BOTTLE TOP / HOLE

4 PAPER CLIP / TOP

5 PLASTICINE WEIGHT / BOTTLE

STICK

YOU WILL NEED:
STRING
STICKY TAPE
A STICK (30 cm LONG)
PAPER CLIP
BOTTLE WITH SCREW TOP
PLASTICINE
CORNER CUT OFF PLASTIC BAG

The weight at the end of the pole balanced the bucket when it was full. The farmer then swung the pole around and emptied the bucket into the canal.

Leather bucket

Kings and their Palaces

The palaces were decorated inside with glazed tiles and stone carvings showing the king's great deeds.

The Assyrians believed that their land belonged to the god Ashur. The king, as Ashur's servant, ruled the land, waged war in his name, built temples and appointed priests and led important religious festivals.

Assyrian kings usually had many wives and children. The son chosen by the king to be his heir was specially educated in the "House of the Succession" to be a good ruler.

This is King Ashurnasirpal II in the throne room of his palace. Here, the king receives royal messengers from all parts of the empire who keep him in touch with what is happening.

Ashurnasirpal and several other kings fought hard to enlarge the empire. To celebrate, they used prisoners of war to build their splendid palaces and cities in Khorsabad, Nineveh and Nimrud.

King's personal servant

Servant carrying the king's weapons

The palace garden

King Ashurbanipal relaxes in his garden with the queen and his servants and musicians.

His garden is planted with exotic trees and flowers gathered from all over the empire.

Musicians

Lion hunting

When not leading the army in war, the king hunted to show his skill and bravery. Lions were brought specially to his hunting parks.

Walls of soldiers with their shields stop the lions escaping.

Lions were kept in cages until the king was ready for them.

King Ashurbanipal

Grape vines

Servants with fans

King

Queen

Furniture decorated with gold and ivory inlays.

The Assyrian Army

1 Going into battle

The Assyrians had to fight continually to keep their empire under control. Here the army is setting out to attack a city which has rebelled against their rule.

The foot soldiers were armed with bows and arrows, slings for hurling stones, or lances. The cavalry, that is the soldiers on horseback, also used bows and lances.

Horse-drawn chariots each carried a team of driver, bowman and shield-bearer. The army also had siege engines which had battering rams and space inside for bowmen.

Sacking the captured city

Often, the Assyrians completely destroyed the captured city and the farmland around it. They took its treasure as booty and either killed the citizens or took them captive.

Houses in the city have been set on fire.

Soldiers knock down the city walls.

Orchards are burnt.

Valuable goods and animals are taken away as booty.

Heads of dead citizens are collected and counted.

Captives are led away.

Some of the captives became slaves, but others were sent to live in new cities. The Assyrians hoped that their experiences would teach them not to rebel again.

The soldiers swam across rivers clutching inflated animal skins to help them keep afloat. The horses swam too. The chariots were rowed across in small round boats.

When they reached the city, heavily armed soldiers scaled the walls with ladders while bowmen and slingers fired from further away. Siege engines battered the wall and gate.

Inside a siege engine

The siege engines were made of wood and covered with animal's skins. They could be pushed up to the city walls with several bowmen hidden inside. The ram was used for breaking down gates and undermining walls.

Holes for firing arrows through.

The engine was moved by soldiers pushing from behind.

The battering ram was raised and lowered by this rope.

Wooden frame

Animal skins

Key dates

2000	**Pazur-Ashur I** reigned about the time Assyria became independent of Sumerian empire.
1814/1782	**Shamsi-Adad I.** First king to extend Assyria's frontiers.
911/891	**Adad-nirari II** united his people.
883/859	**Ashurnasirpal II**
858/824	**Shalmaneser III**
721/705	**Sargon II**
704/681	**Sennacherib**
668/631	**Ashurbanipal**
614/609	Complete destruction of empire.

Approximate BC dates

The conquered people

Local prince

Assyrian official

Conspirators planning rebellion

Some conquered lands, such as Egypt, were ruled by local princes, but Assyrian officials stayed to make sure they were loyal. Even so, as the empire grew, rebellions were common.

Assyrian scribe

People bringing tribute

Conquered people had to pay tribute to the Assyrians. Failure to do so was rapidly punished and the Assyrians were notorious for the cruel tortures they inflicted on people.

The City of Babylon

The ancient city of Babylon stood on the banks of the River Euphrates. Under its great king, Hammurabi, Babylon controlled an empire, but this gradually broke up after he died about 1750BC.

For several hundred years Babylon was ruled peacefully by a people called the Kassites. In 1171BC, the Kassites were driven out by the Elamites. A troubled time followed. The Assyrians then claimed to rule Babylon, but some Babylonians resisted them.

The marshes of southern Mesopotamia made a good hiding place for Babylonians fighting against Assyrian rule. One of their leaders was Merodach-Baladan.

With the help of their neighbours, the Medes, the Babylonians defeated the Assyrians in 612BC. Nebuchadnezzar, the son of their general, went on to win an empire.

Telling the future

The Babylonians believed they could tell the future by looking at a sheep's liver. This clay model was made as a guide to the different parts for the priests to look at.

Key dates

1500/1350	The Kassites ruled in peace. After 1350 there were wars with the Elamites and Assyrians.
1171	Kassite rule ended by Elamites.
729	**Tiglathpileser** of Assyria became king of Babylon.
721/711	**Merodach-Baladan** led resistance to Assyria.
689	**Sennacherib** of Assyria destroyed Babylon.
626/605	**Nabopolassar** led fight against Assyrians, with help of Medes.
605/562	**Nebuchadnezzar** ruled Babylon.
556/539	**Nabonidus** ruled Babylon.
539	Babylon captured by Persians.
Approximate BC dates	

Ishtar Gate

Part of the New Year procession

Processional Way

The city of Babylon was rebuilt by Nebuchadnezzar and it became one of the richest cities in the world. The city was entered through a huge gateway, covered with glazed blue tiles, called the Ishtar Gate. Nearby was Nebuchadnezzar's magnificent palace, with its famous Hanging Garden.

Courtyard houses

This huge ziggurat and temple, which Nebuchadnezzar built, was dedicated to the Babylonians' chief god, Marduk.

Nebuchadnezzar's palace

Water from the river was used to water the Hanging Gardens.

These are the Hanging Gardens of Babylon. They were built by Nebuchadnezzar for his wife Amytis, a princess of the Medes, because she missed the hilly landscape of her home.

Processional Way

The people of Babylon are watching a procession make its way to the temple of Marduk for the New Year festival. Old traditions like this were revived when Babylon was rebuilt.

City walls

The goddess Ishtar

This is a statue of Ishtar, the chief goddess of Babylon after whom the great gate was named. It is carved from alabaster and has rubies inlaid in it.

The end of Babylon

Royal Persian Guardsmen

In 539BC, Babylon was taken over by the Persians whose power was rapidly increasing. People gradually left the city and by AD200, it was deserted and ruined.

59

Monument Builders

The climate of North Europe is so damp that things buried in the ground decay quickly and leave little trace for archaeologists. Because of this we know less about the people of Europe than about the people of the Middle East. No texts have been found, so we do not know if they could write. From very early times, however, people in Europe built great stone monuments, and the treasures that have survived show they were highly skilled craftsmen.

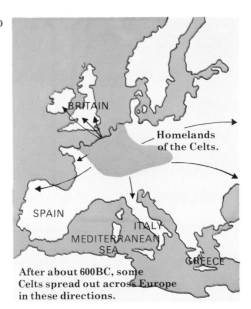

After about 600BC, some Celts spread out across Europe in these directions.

Treasures of Europe

These are just a few examples of the fine craftsmanship of the people living in Europe in ancient times.

Rock carvings like this were found in Sweden and Norway. They often show ships carrying the sun across the sky.

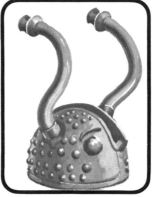

This bronze helmet is from Vixo in Denmark. It was probably not worn in battle because it is too heavy and awkward.

This is a bronze model of a chariot carrying the sun. It was thrown into a marsh in Denmark as an offering to the gods.

Metalworkers in Europe were very skilled. This helmet and armour came from Villanova in Italy.

This enormous bronze wine jar was made in Greece and then taken to France. It was buried in the grave of a princess.

Building Stonehenge

The most impressive of the ancient stone circles is Stonehenge in southern England. Work began on it about 2750BC. It was changed several times and here the last and most impressive version is being built. It was finished soon after 1500BC.

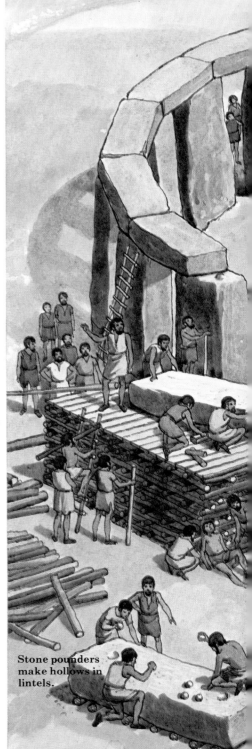

Stone pounders make hollows in lintels.

About a thousand men are needed to pull one of the sarsen stones from the quarry over 32km away.

This is Stonehenge when it was completed. It was probably a temple but some scholars think it was also used as a calendar.

Lintel

Blue-stones

Sarsen

These "bluestones" were brought from Wales and were used in an earlier stone circle. When this circle is finished, they will be put in the middle of it.

Wooden rollers are placed under the sledge to make it move more easily.

Sarsen being raised into position in its hole.

Sledge

These lumps fit in hollows on lintels.

The upright stones are called sarsens.

Tree-trunk lever

The chalky earth is taken away in baskets.

Pick made of antler.

These men are digging a hole for the next sarsen.

The lintels are lifted up on towers of logs placed criss-cross. The layers of logs are slipped under the stone one at a time to gradually raise the lintel to the top of the sarsens.

First Civilisation in China

Civilisation in China began near the Yellow River. Here, the Shang kings ruled for about 500 years, until a war-like people called the Chou conquered them in 1057BC.

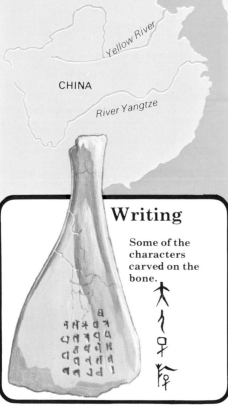

The kings lived in palaces built of wood and earth.

The first farmers of northern China grew millet and kept cattle and pigs. They probably lived in pit houses dug out of the ground.

Pit houses with thatched roofs.

A Chou noble drives away from the king's palace in his war chariot. The chariot had no seat, just a platform to stand on.

Writing

Some of the characters carved on the bone.

The earliest form of Chinese writing is found cut into animal bones. These were used for taking messages which were thought to come from the gods.

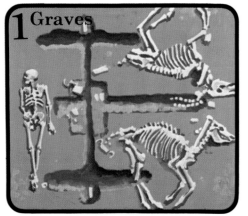

1 Graves

Recently the Chinese opened the tombs of the Shang kings near Anyang. They found the skeletons of horses and charioteers with their chariots.

2

The Shang king thought his ancestors were gods. He offered them meat and wine in bronze vessels like this one. Many Chinese still honour their ancestors today.

3

Jade ornaments like this animal were sewn to the dead person's clothes. Objects like this ornamental dagger were put in the graves of nobles and rich people.

First Farmers in America

Many different tribes lived in Central and Southern America. It seems that they became farmers later than the people in the Middle East.

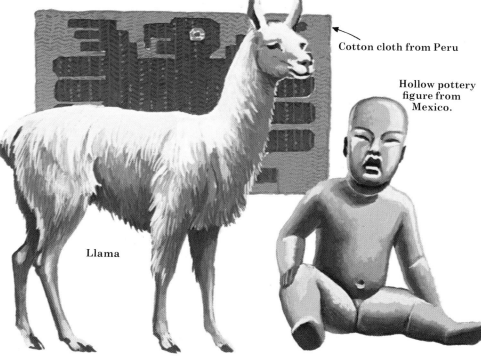

Cotton cloth from Peru

Hollow pottery figure from Mexico.

Llama

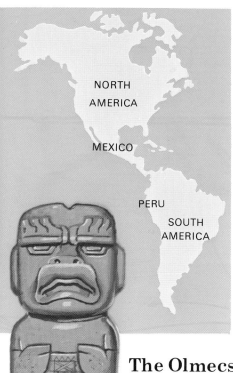

NORTH AMERICA

MEXICO

PERU

SOUTH AMERICA

The farmers had been growing cotton since 3000BC. They spun and wove it by hand to make cloth with special designs like the one here. They got wool from llamas and alpacas.

Their most important crop was maize, which first appeared in Mexico in 2500BC. Pottery, like this figure was being made from 2300BC onwards.

The Olmecs

The Olmecs, first of the famous cultures of this area, appear about 1200BC. You can recognize their statues and jade and pottery figures by their "baby" faces.

Olmec carving made of jade.

In Mexico, the Olmecs were building shrines on great mounds like this by 600BC. At this time they had no wheels or metal tools, so the buildings were an amazing achievement.

India

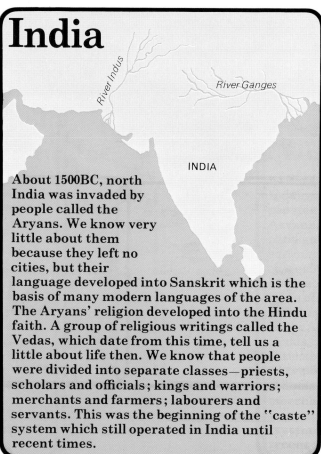

River Indus

River Ganges

INDIA

About 1500BC, north India was invaded by people called the Aryans. We know very little about them because they left no cities, but their language developed into Sanskrit which is the basis of many modern languages of the area. The Aryans' religion developed into the Hindu faith. A group of religious writings called the Vedas, which date from this time, tell us a little about life then. We know that people were divided into separate classes—priests, scholars and officials; kings and warriors; merchants and farmers; labourers and servants. This was the beginning of the "caste" system which still operated in India until recent times.

The Dark Ages

The years 1100 to 700BC in Greece are called the Dark Ages as so little is known about them. New people called the Dorians invaded and after that no more great palaces were built. People lived simply. They burnt their dead instead of burying them with offerings.

.It was now easier to get iron, so people could make strong tools and weapons. Greece was divided into several city-states, such as Corinth, Athens and Sparta, which often quarrelled amongst themselves.

This is Homer, who composed poems about the siege of Troy and the adventures of a hero called Odysseus. His poems were passed on by word of mouth for years until writing came into use again.

Greek letters

ABEKMNRT

ABEKMNRT

Our letters

The Greeks took over the Phoenician alphabet and adapted it to suit their own needs. It was so simple to use that many people could learn to read and write.

As the numbers of people grew, many went abroad. Some set up colonies in other countries and traded. Others hired themselves out to foreign kings as soldiers.

The Greeks were the first people to make coins of a standard weight and quality of metal. These made trade much easier and the traders became very rich.

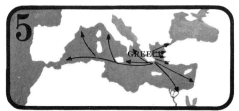

By trading and setting up colonies around the Mediterranean, the Greeks grew prosperous. They became dangerous competitors for the Phoenician merchants.

Soldiers

These are Greek soldiers called Hoplites. They fought in closely packed ranks, each man protecting the one next to him with his shield.

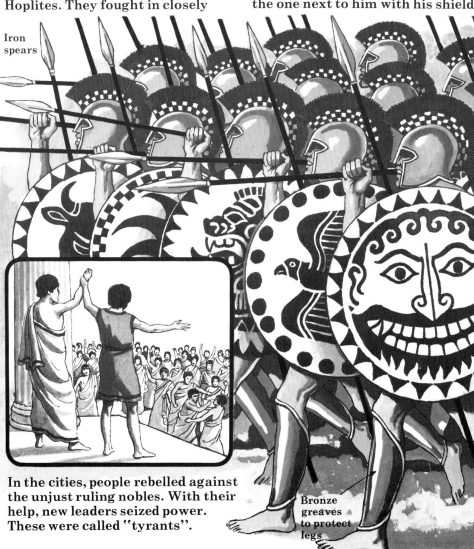

Iron spears

Bronze greaves to protect legs

In the cities, people rebelled against the unjust ruling nobles. With their help, new leaders seized power. These were called "tyrants".

64

Conquerors

The land we now call Iran was invaded by new people about 1200BC. The invaders seem to have come from somewhere in Europe, like many others who arrived in the Middle East from 2000BC onwards.

One Iranian tribe, called the Medes, became powerful and in 612BC helped to destroy the empire of the Assyrians. Another group was the Persians, who later took over the Babylonian empire. Led by a great king called Cyrus, the Persians then won a huge empire of their own.

Persepolis

King Darius, a successor of Cyrus began building an enormous palace at Persepolis in 518BC. The great hall, shown here, was big enough to hold 10,000 people.

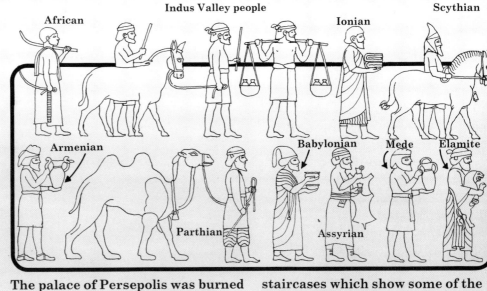

The palace of Persepolis was burned down in 330BC by Alexander the Great, but some of the carvings survived. These pictures are of carvings on one of the great staircases which show some of the people conquered by the Persians. They are bringing horses, camels, skins, cloth and gold as tribute to the Persian king.

Visitors were led through many halls and terraces which were decorated with stone carvings. The palace does not seem to have been lived in by the kings. It was probably used for special ceremonies like the celebration of the New Year.

Here, important Persians and Medes wait to be received by the king.

65

The Persian Empire

The great Persian king, Darius I, ran his empire cleverly and efficiently. He collected taxes from all the conquered people, but allowed them to keep their own customs, religions and way of life as long as they were obedient. Darius appointed local governors, called satraps, to rule the provinces of the empire and used Persian soldiers to check that the satraps did not become too powerful. He also had good roads built so that messengers could travel quickly with news from all over the empire.

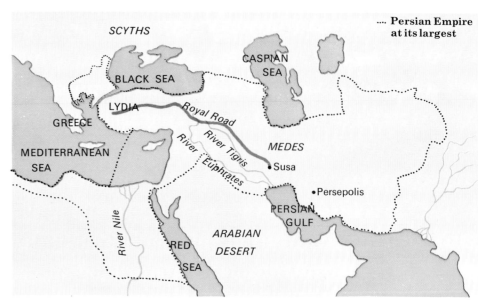

.... Persian Empire at its largest

SCYTHS · CASPIAN SEA · BLACK SEA · LYDIA · Royal Road · River Tigris · River Euphrates · MEDES · GREECE · MEDITERRANEAN SEA · Susa · Persepolis · River Nile · PERSIAN GULF · ARABIAN DESERT · RED SEA

1 The Crown Prince, Xerxes · King Darius I · Visitors must not go past this point. · Incense burners

The Persians lived in the land we now call Iran. They won a huge empire under their great king, Cyrus, whose successor, King Darius I, is shown here.

Darius organised the empire very efficiently. He appointed local governors, called satraps, to rule each province and used Persian soldiers to check that they did not

become too powerful. He also had good roads built so that messengers could travel quickly with news from all over the empire.

2

As long as conquered people paid their taxes, the Persians treated them and their customs with respect. Here, officials check tax payments before storing them in the palace.

Religion

Fire was sacred to the Persians and the Magi (priests) kept one burning on an altar. A prophet, Zarathushtra, changed Persian religion from the worship of many gods to that of one, Ahuramazda.

Key dates

2000/1800	The Aryans migrated from southern Russia
628	Birth of **Zarathushtra** religious prophet.
559/529	Reign of **Cyrus the Great.**
547	**Cyrus** defeated King Croesus of Lydia.
521/486	Reign of **Darius I.**
513/512	First Asian invasion of Europe. Persians conquered Thrace and Macedon.
490	Persians defeated by Greeks at Battle of Marathon.
486/465	Reign of **Xerxes I**, son of Darius.
480	Persians defeated by Greeks at Salamis.
330	**Alexander** destroyed Persian Empire. Persepolis was burned.

Approximate BC dates

The Greeks at War

Until 1100BC, the Mycenaeans ruled Greece. Then the Dorians invaded and a troubled time followed when wealth and culture declined. We call this the Greek Dark Ages. Later prosperity gradually returned.

Meanwhile, the Persian empire was growing rapidly. The Persians conquered Lydia, until then a Greek area ruled by King Croesus, and forced the Greek cities there to pay "tribute" (a kind of tax) to them. Later, several of these cities, led by Athens, rebelled and the so-called "Persian Wars" began.

1 The Persian king, Darius I, invaded Greece, but was defeated at Marathon in 490BC. The news was carried over 40km to Athens by a runner. Our Olympic marathon race is named after this.

2 War with Greece was continued by Darius' son Xerxes. He built a bridge of boats to get his army across the Hellespont, using ropes and ships made by his Egyptian and Phoenician subjects.

3 The Athenians discovered a rich vein of silver in their mines and so had money to build a new fleet. They finally defeated the Persians in a battle off the coast of Salamis.

4 Athens became the greatest city of Greece. It led a league of Greek cities which were afraid that the Persians might attack again, and collected money from them.

Athens' great leader Pericles built these fine new buildings to replace those damaged in the Persian wars. The other cities were angry because he used money belonging to the league to build them.

Spartan soldiers

5 The state of Sparta led the enemies of Athens in a long and terrible war, known as the Peloponnesian War. It lasted 27 years until Athens was defeated in 404BC.

Life in Athens

Town life almost disappeared in Greece during the Dark Ages, but as trade slowly increased, the cities grew again. A city and the land around it formed a city-state. The largest and most famous of these was Athens. It had a high place, called the Acropolis, where the people could go in times of danger. All the "citizens", that is all the free men, not women or slaves, took part in the running of the city by voting on important matters. This is called democracy and it was first used in Athens.

The Parthenon temple, built by Pericles for the goddess Athena.

The old city, called the Acropolis.

The Sacred Way which leads to the Acropolis.

The Agora where people met to argue about politics and buy and sell things.

Open-air restaurant

Grape vines

Potter high-c

Trade with Athens

Piraeus, the port of Athens, is about six kilometres away. Goods from all over the Mediterranean were landed there, including wine from the Aegean islands and grain from the Black Sea ports.

Theatre

Stage

Actors

Chorus

Altar

Orchestra

Padded actor from wall painting

Pottery copy of actor's mask

A Greek theatre had a round area called the orchestra where the actors performed. The audience often brought cushions to sit on because the seats were stone.

The idea of the theatre grew from dances held at festivals in honour of the gods. Later, writers like Euripedes and Sophocles produced plays specially for the theatre.

All the parts in plays were taken by men who wore masks and padding. Copies of the masks were made in pottery to decorate building

Politics

Discs meaning "guilty"

Disc meaning "not guilty"

Ostraka

Politician's name

All "citizens" discussed and voted on city matters. Our word "politics" comes from the Greek *politikos*, which means "of the city".

There were no lawyers, so people had to present their own cases in court. Jurors showed their verdicts with small discs like these.

A politician could be sent into exile if 6,000 citizens wrote his name on pieces of broken pottery like these, called ostraka.

The philosopher Socrates was condemned because some people feared the way he questioned everything. He chose to die and drank poison.

Potters' workshop

Potters' quarter of city

Pottery

Athens was famous for its pottery. Everyday things, like this baby's bottle and toy, were made of pottery, as well as fine vases painted with scenes of gods and heroes or daily life.

How we know

The scenes painted on vases tell us a lot about Greek life. This one shows a boy buying new sandals. He places his foot on the leather and the shoemaker cuts round it.

These women are celebrating the festival of the god Dionysus with wild dances. Most of the time women stayed at home and did not take part in public life.

Boys were well educated from the age of seven. This boy is learning to read. Music and sports were also taught. Girls stayed at home and were taught by their mothers.

Alexander the Great

The Greek city-states still quarrelled among themselves even when the Peloponnesian War was over. Peace was not restored until Philip, King of Macedon took control. The Greeks thought him a barbarian, which to them was anyone who was not Greek. Philip wanted to fight the Persians with Greek help. but he died leaving his son, Alexander, to carry out his plan. Alexander set out to conquer an empire.

1 Alexander was educated in the Greek way by the philosopher Aristotle. Like all Macedonians, though, he was a tough soldier.

2 Alexander crossed into Asia with his army and defeated the Persian king Darius III at the battle of Issus in 333BC. This Roman mosaic is a copy of a Greek painting showing Alexander at Issus.

3 He moved on through the Persian empire to Syria. The Phoenician city of Tyre was attacked with catapults on boats.

4 Egypt was easily conquered. Here, at the oasis of Siwa, Alexander was hailed as the son of the god Ammon. Some Greeks disapproved of this.

5 Alexander fought Darius again and finally defeated him in 331BC. Then he led his army through difficult mountainous country to Persepolis.

6 The Persian king's treasure was stored at Persepolis. Alexander's army captured and looted it and then set off towards India.

7 When they arrived in India, they won many battles, including one against King Porus, in which they met war elephants for the first time.

8 Alexander died of a fever in 323BC on the long trek home from India. His body was taken to Alexandria in Egypt and buried there.

Alexandria

Alexander founded many cities, all called Alexandria after him. The greatest of all was on the Mediterranean coast of Egypt. It became one of the most splendid cities of the ancient world. Alexander's general, Ptolemy, became King of Egypt and founded the Mouseion, a place where scholars could meet, talk and do scientific experiments. There was also a magnificent library containing many valuable books. Ptolemy's family ruled Egypt for 300 years.

Bronze mirrors at the top reflected the light.

The Pharos

Many buildings were of Greek design with columns and statues.

Some Egyptian monuments, like this obelisk, were also erected.

The lighthouse of Alexandria, the Pharos, was one of the wonders of the world. Alexandrian merchants sailed to India and the East, bringing back spices and silks for sale in the Mediterranean world.

Science and inventions

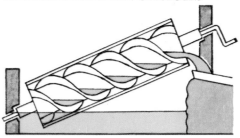

Many things were invented in Alexandria. Archimedes is said to have designed this screw, which lifts water from one level to another. It is still used today.

An astronomer called Ptolemy studied the planets from Alexandria. He believed the Earth was the centre of the universe as he showed in this diagram.

The Alexandrians were interested in geography. This is the scientist Eratosthenes who used the angle of the sun's shadow to work out the distance round the Earth.

Siege catapult

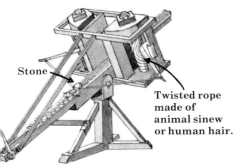

Stone

Twisted rope made of animal sinew or human hair.

Alexander's military engineers designed catapults, which hurled stones, for attacking walled cities. Later, the Romans used catapults in their sieges too.

How to make a catapult

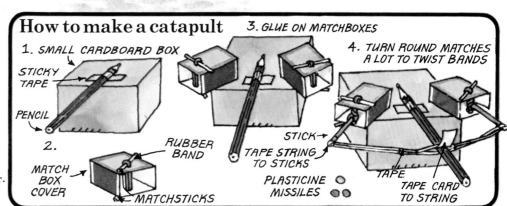

1. SMALL CARDBOARD BOX
STICKY TAPE
PENCIL
2.
MATCH BOX COVER
RUBBER BAND
MATCHSTICKS
3. GLUE ON MATCHBOXES
4. TURN ROUND MATCHES A LOT TO TWIST BANDS
STICK
TAPE STRING TO STICKS
PLASTICINE MISSILES
TAPE
TAPE CARD TO STRING

Stick a pencil to a small box, like this. Make holes through two matchbox covers, push through short rubber bands. Slide match sticks through them. Glue covers to the box.

Push two sticks into the bands. Tape string to the ends. Tape the string on each side of the pencil and a bit of card on top. Wind round the match sticks. Load and pull back to fire.

What We Owe the Greeks

We know more about the Greeks than many earlier people, because they wrote proper histories. Other people listed kings' names and events, but did not try to explain things. The Greek historian, Herodotus, wrote studies of people and their customs. Thucydides, who fought in the Peloponnesian War, wrote a detailed history of the war and its causes. Besides the writing of history, we have inherited many other things from the Greeks, including ideas of politics, theatre and many words.

The Greeks developed the art of thinking about problems. They called this philosophy. Two of the world's greatest philosophers, Socrates and Plato, lived in Athens.

Some scholars, like Aristotle, studied scientific problems. He carefully watched animals and realised that the porpoise was a mammal not a fish when he saw it give birth to live babies.

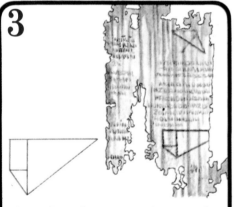

The rules of geometry invented by Greeks such as Euclid and Pythagoras are still used today. This Greek papyrus shows how to solve a problem in geometry.

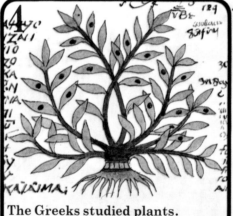

The Greeks studied plants. Manuscripts, like this, record recipes for medicines made of plants. Alexander sent rare plants from the East to Aristotle.

Chariot racing

The Olympic Games

Greek festivals held in honour of the gods included competitions in sports, music and drama. Some of these "games" lasted several days. The games at Corinth and the Pythian Games at Delphi were both important, but the most famous were the Olympic Games held every four years at the great sanctuary of the god Zeus at Olympia.

The competitors had to be free Greeks, not slaves, and they swore an oath to keep the rules. All wars in Greece had to stop while the games were in progress. At the end of the games, oxen were sacrificed to Zeus and everyone joined in a great feast.

Discus

Temple of Zeus

This athlete is about to throw a round bronze weight called the discus. The winner is the man who throws it furthest.

Art and architecture

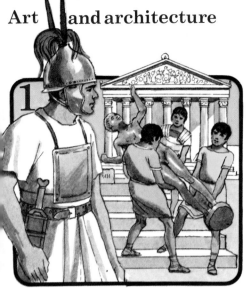

1 When the Romans conquered Greece, their generals carried off many works of art. The Romans admired Greek statues so much that they had marble copies made.

2 After the fall of the Roman empire, statues were buried and lost. In the 15th century AD, people began to be interested in the ancient world and dug up the remains.

3 From then on, architects throughout Europe revived Greek and Roman styles of building. Today, most cities have some public buildings which are in the "Classical" style.

Throwing the javelin. It was hurled from a leather thong wrapped round the athlete's fingers.

Four-horse racing was part of the Olympic Games, but it took place on a separate race-track called the hippodrome. The Romans took over this exciting sport from the Greeks.

Wrestling

Judge with his official rod

This is a sprint race. There were also races run by men wearing full armour.

Spot the columns

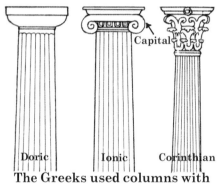

Doric   Ionic   Corinthian

Capital

The Greeks used columns with decorated tops (capitals) to support the roofs of their temples. You may be able to spot these columns on present-day buildings.

Key dates

499	Ionian Greeks revolted against Persian rule.
490	Start of Persian wars. Persians defeated at Battle of Marathon.
480	Greeks defeated at Thermopylae, then victorious at Salamis.
478/477	Athens led league of Greek states.
462/429	**Pericles,** leader at Athens.
431/404	**Peloponnesian War** between Sparta and Athens.
338	**Philip II** of Macedon won control of Greece.
336/323	**Reign of Alexander the Great.** During this time Alexander won a huge empire. On his death, the empire was divided up by his successors.

Approximate BC dates.

Great Civilisation in the East

Until 221BC, China was divided into several rival states. Then, the king of a state called Ch'in defeated them all and became the First Emperor of all China. "Shih Huang Ti", as he was called, was the first of a family line of emperors (a dynasty) called the Ch'in emperors.

Later, a new dynasty of emperors—the Han emperors—ruled China. During their time, General Chang Chien was sent to the West to find allies. As a result of his travels, a new trade route, called the Silk Road, was opened up.

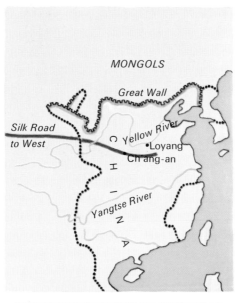

Key dates

551/479BC	The great thinker **Confucius**.
463/221BC	Period of the warring states.
221BC	China unified under **Shih Huang Ti**, the first emperor. Great Wall built. Beginning of Ch'in Dynasty. Standard bronze coins introduced.
206BC/AD220	Han Dynasty.
200BC*	Paper invented. Beginnings of Chinese civil service.

***These dates are approximate**

When the people of China were counted in AD2, there were about 60 million. Most were peasants who grew rice, their most important crop, on specially built terraces.

The great lords had huge tombs built for themselves for a comfortable life-after-death. This princess's body was covered with jade, which was thought to preserve it.

The emperor was the supreme lord. He controlled the salt wells, which were vital to people far from the sea. Bamboo tubes were drilled down 400 metres into the brine.

How we know

Peasant's cottage

Peasant girl

We can learn a great deal about life at the time of the Han emperors from the pottery models placed in tombs. This is a simple one-storey house a peasant might live in.

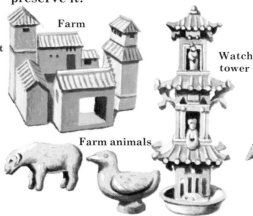

Farm

Watch tower

Farm animals

In troubled times, even a farm needed towers to watch for barbarians or soldiers. A rich lord had models of servants and soldiers in his tomb to impress the gods.

Bronze figure of tall Western horse

General Chang Chien brought back a new breed of horses from the West. The big, strong horses were very useful against the small ponies ridden by the barbarians.

forced to work on this largest
construction ever put up.

The Great Wall

The Great Wall of China was built
by Shih Huang Ti when he became
emperor. He joined together short
sections of wall put up by
earlier warlords to keep
raiding tribes out of their
lands. The wall still stands
and is 2,710km long.

Beacons on the watch
towers signal the
approach of an enemy.

A convoy on
the Silk Road is
halted by an
attack.

Chinese
cross-bowman

Barbarians on
their swift
ponies.

The wall is wide
enough to take
chariots.

Silk

Silkworm

Sorting cocoons

The Chinese made and sold fine silk.
They kept silk worms (caterpillars of
the silk moth), which spin cocoons
of fine silk thread. They dyed
and wove this silk into cloth.

Patterns of plants and animals
were woven into the silk. This lion
pattern may have been borrowed
from Persia, which shows ideas as
well as goods were taken along the
Silk Road.

Money

Fish
money

Standard
money

Silk

Silk was so valuable it could be
used for payment. Bronze coins in
strange shapes were also used.
Later, round coins with square
holes became the standard money.

Writing and Inventions

The Chinese emperor was treated almost like a god by his millions of subjects. He had armies of officials and soldiers to run his empire. The officials—civil servants—collected taxes and looked after roads.

People who wanted to be civil servants had to take exams. Any boy who could read and write had a chance. But he had to know large amounts of ancient poetry and the teachings of the great thinker, Confucius.

Confucius was born in 551BC. He taught that the emperor should be like a father to his people who should love and obey him. Confucia scholars had to be good at music, arithmetic, archery and chess.

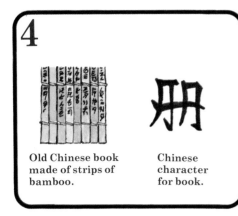

Old Chinese book made of strips of bamboo.

Chinese character for book.

The writing used in China today is thousands of years old. Each character was based on a picture. Gradually the pictures became simple brush strokes.

The ancient Chinese wrote and painted on long pieces of silk. They used Chinese brushes and ground up a solid block of ink on a stone with a little water.

The Chinese painted pictures in beautiful colours. In a corner, they often put the characters which were based on things in the picture, such as "mountain" and "river".

Make a Chinese wall-hanging

You will need a piece of paper about foolscap size. Fasten a piece of cane at each end with sticky tape. Hold your brush in the Chinese way and paint a landscape picture, using the Chinese painting above as a guide. Next copy the Chinese characters. These are the characters for "river" and "mountain". Together they mean "landscape".

Inventions

At first the Chinese wrote on costly silk or in heavy bamboo books. Later, they began making paper from bark and hemp. This was used for writing, painting and taking rubbings from stone tablets.

Life in the city

All the cities built at the time of the Han emperors have disappeared. This picture of their capital city, Ch'ang-An, is based on details from paintings, sculptures and tomb figures made at the time.

A rich merchant lives in this splendid painted house with his family and slaves.

An elegant procession of court officials.

A scholar teaches his pupils the ideas of Confucius. People respect scholars much more than rich merchants.

House walls are lacquered to make them waterproof.

People buy food at market stalls.

A government official rides in his carriage. He is very important and people have to jump out of the way.

2

The Chinese invented the first compass. A spoon-shaped piece of magnetic stone, called lode stone, was placed on a polished bronze board. The spoon turned until it pointed to the North Pole.

3

The Chinese covered wooden bowls and boxes with layers of sticky resin, called lacquer, from the lac tree. They lacquered their shoes, chariots and umbrellas to make them waterproof and colourful.

4

This is an instrument for detecting earthquakes. The slightest tremor in the earth tilts the carefully balanced mechanism inside. Then a dragon's jaws open and a ball falls into a toad's mouth.

Nomads and Horsemen

Between the civilisations of the Mediterranean and China were vast treeless plains and mountains. The tribes living there wandered great distances to find pasture for their horses and cattle.

One tribe, the Mongols, sometimes attacked the Great Wall of China. Another, the Scythians, were described by the Greek historian, Herodotus, as fine horsemen and archers. Russians digging in the Altai found tombs built about 500BC with objects preserved in ice.

MONGOLS

ALTAI

SCYTHS

ARAL SEA

BLACK SEA

CASPIAN SEA

PERSIANS

Zagros Mountains

CHINA

Himalayas

RED SEA

PERSIAN GULF

INDIA

Scythian horse-breeders

The Scythians of the Altai roamed the plains during the summer months but lived in log cabins during the winter. They sold horses from their huge herds to the Chinese and Persians.

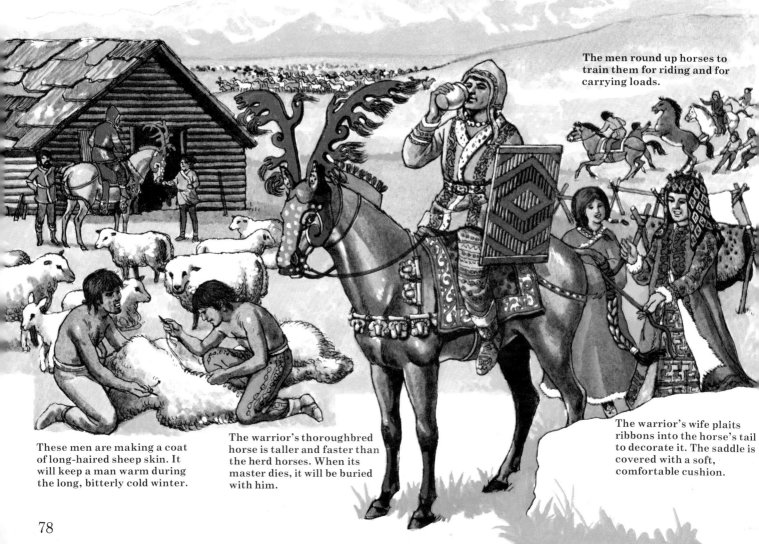

The men round up horses to train them for riding and for carrying loads.

These men are making a coat of long-haired sheep skin. It will keep a man warm during the long, bitterly cold winter.

The warrior's thoroughbred horse is taller and faster than the herd horses. When its master dies, it will be buried with him.

The warrior's wife plaits ribbons into the horse's tail to decorate it. The saddle is covered with a soft, comfortable cushion.

Inside a Scythian cabin

During the winter, the Scythians made things of felt, with cut-out shapes sewn on them, called appliqué. They also stitched embroidery. All their belongings were made so that they could be packed on to horses when they moved on.

How to do appliqué

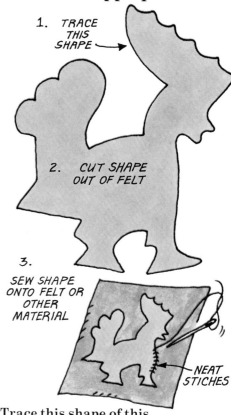

1. TRACE THIS SHAPE

2. CUT SHAPE OUT OF FELT

3. SEW SHAPE ONTO FELT OR OTHER MATERIAL

NEAT STICHES

Trace this shape of this Scythian cockerel and cut it out of coloured felt or material. Stitch it to a large piece of felt or cloth. Sew on more cut-out shapes to make a wall hanging.

1 Mongols

The Mongols were true nomads and wandered the whole year round. Their tents, called yurts, were made of animal hair felt, waterproofed with fat, and held up by wooden frames.

2

Mongol chieftains had very large yurts, comfortably furnished inside. They loaded them on to large carts, pulled by teams of oxen, when it was time to drive their herds on again.

How we know

The Scythians made things of gold, such as this plaque. It may show a warrior's death.

3

When ponies were needed from the herd, men caught them with lassoos on poles. The men made a special drink of mares' milk but most work was done by women.

4

Water was so precious to the Mongols when travelling that no cooking pots or clothes were allowed to be washed. Visitors to a camp had to walk between fires to be purified.

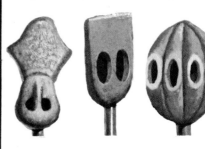

The Mongols made whistles, like these to join to arrows. They could hear where an arrow fell.

Early American Indians

The first "Indians" of North America ate seeds and berries, and followed herds of wild animals. Later, they began to build more permanent homes and grow crops near them.

Some, like the Hopewell people, built large cemeteries for their dead. In Central America the Indians began to build pyramids. At first they faced them with clay and later with stone slabs. Ideas and knowledge spread, partly when they traded with each other, back from Mexico to the Indians of North America.

NORTHERN FOREST TRIBES

NORTH AMERICA

CENTRAL AMERICA

TRIBES OF THE GREAT PLAINS

EASTERN WOODLAND TRIBES

SOUTH WEST DESERT TRIBES

•Serpent Mound

SOUTH EAST AND FLORIDA TRIBES

SOUTH WEST MESA TRIBES

ATLANTIC OCEAN

PACIFIC OCEAN

Teotihuacan

OLMECS

MEXICO

MAYA

•Copan

The Indians of the desert lived in caves and went out hunting for wild sheep. They wove elaborate baskets and the mocassins they made of skins have been found.

On the plains and in the woodlands, the Indians lived in shallow pit houses, covered with hides. A holy man, called a shaman, chanted spells to cure ill people.

Some of the woodland tribes built huge mounds of earth in the shape of animals. This snake is about 500 metres long and was made by Hopewell Indians 2,000 years ago.

Olmec Indians in Central America built huge stone statues. This one is three metres high. They thought their jaguar-god mated with women, who had half-jaguar babies.

A city of pyramids was built at Teotihuacan in Central Mexico. Round the city were fields of maize, beans and pumpkins to feed about 200,000 people who lived there.

Maize god   Maize plant

The Indians of North America learned how to grow tobacco from the people in Central America. They also grew maize, which came from Mexico. It was such a good food, they made it a god.

The Maya

The Maya Indians of Central America built cities which can still be seen deep in the jungle. They were a very religious people and worshipped rain, earth, plant and animal gods. They played a religious ball game in specially built courts. Priests helped the players to dress and kept score.

The Maya studied the moon, stars and planets, and had a complicated calendar for counting the days and years. They wanted to predict when such frightening things as an eclipse of the sun would happen.

How to play hip ball

A player tosses the ball over the line. The teams hit it across the line, using only hips, thighs and elbows. A point is scored against the one who lets it drop. The first to score 21 wins the game.

The ball court at Copan

The ball court at Copan was probably built late in the eighth century AD. The players, bandaged to prevent injuries, used a solid rubber ball.

They bounced the ball backwards and forwards, using only their hips, thighs and elbows, but not their feet. No one really knows how they scored goals.

How we know

We know very little about how the Maya people lived. This tomb painting shows they fought their neighbours, probably to capture people to sacrifice to the gods.

The Maya were very good stone carvers. These masons are working on a giant pillar, probably showing a king, which will be set up to mark an important date in the calendar.

Maya pot showing bat god.

Mayan potters made marvellous pots of clay. They coiled long strips of clay round and round, to build up the pot. The man here turns the pot round with his feet.

Life in Ancient Africa

The first people lived in Africa about three million years ago. From the great civilisations of Egypt, other Africans learned how to work gold, copper, tin and bronze.

The Assyrians, with iron weapons, invaded the Nile valley in 671BC and the use of iron spread. Two powerful kingdoms grew up south of Egypt—Kush and Axum (modern Ethiopia). Christianity was brought to Ethiopia by Egyptian monks. King Ezana was one of the first rulers to become a Christian.

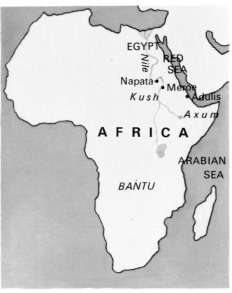

Key dates

1000BC*	Beginnings of Kingdom of Kush. Capital at Napata.
751/664BC	Kushite kings conquered and and ruled Egypt.
671BC	The Asyrians invaded the Nile Valley.
590BC*	Capital of Kush moved from Napata to Meroe.
AD339	Meroe conquered by King Ezana of Axum.

*These dates are approximate.

Some of Africa's earliest history can be seen in paintings on the walls of caves. This picture, based on a rock painting, shows a battle between small bushmen and tall

Bantu warriors. Such battles between the tribes forced the weaker ones to move their herds and villages to new areas where no people had ever lived before.

The capital of the kingdom of Kush was at Napata until about 590BC. Then a new capital was built at Meroe, near iron deposits. It had pyramid tombs like those in Egypt.

The working of iron probably spread from the kingdom of Kush westwards across Africa. Black-smiths became important because they knew how to make weapons.

The North African coast had been settled by Phoenicians and Greeks. The Romans then went further inland. Nomads in the hills learned to trade at markets.

The traders of Axum exchanged their goods at the port of Adulis. Spices came from India and Ceylon, and cloth from the Roman empire. Romans, Greeks and Arabs bought African ivory.

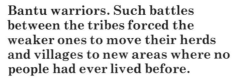

82

Buddha and Ashoka

People called the Aryans moved into India in about 1750BC but little is known of India's history at that time. After the conquests of Alexander the Great in Northern India and Pakistan, a line of kings, the Mauryas, built a great empire. They learned ideas of government from the Greeks and Persians. Ashoka, a Mauryan conqueror, was converted to Buddhism and made it the state religion. Beautiful art and sculpture developed under the next strong line of kings, the Guptas.

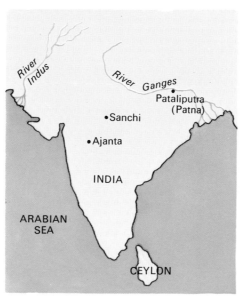

Key dates

560/480BC **Gautama** (The Buddha)
327/325BC Campaigns of Alexander the Great in India and Pakistan.
321/185BC The Mauryan Dynasty founded by **Chandragupta**.
272/231BC **Ashoka**, grandson of Chandragupta, was emperor. Capital city at Pataliputra (modern Patna). Buddhism spread through India.
AD320/535 The Gupta empire.
AD400/500 The Ajanta frescoes were painted.

1 Vishnu one of the many Hindu gods.

The Aryans' religion was Hinduism. Priests taught that the gods decided which way of life, or caste, a person was born into. A good man might be reborn into a better caste.

2 There were four castes, but many people, like those here, were too lowly to be in any of them. They were called "untouchables" and did the worst jobs.

3 The high caste rulers of India lived in great luxury in their palaces. This fresco, painted on a cave wall at Ajanta in about AD400, shows the inside of a palace.

1 Buddha

Gautama, a young prince, was so moved when he saw suffering people, he left his father's palace to find a better way of life.

2 He went to live in a forest as a holy man and thought out a kinder religion. He became known as the Buddha, which means the enlightened one.

3 People listened to the Buddha and his ideas spread. Later, great earth mounds, called stupas, were built in places where he had preached.

4 Top of one of Ashoka's columns.

The Buddha's teachings were adopted by the great Emperor Ashoka. He made fairer laws which were written on stone columns.

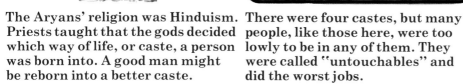

People of Northern Europe

The Celtic tribes moved out from their homelands in north Europe and settled over a wide area. They were fierce warriors, who won the respect of the Greeks and the Romans. Julius Caesar had to fight many hard battles between 58 and 51BC to conquer the Celts in Gaul (now approximately modern France).

The Celts in Britain were not conquered until the invasion of Emperor Claudius in AD43. Even then, they kept their own languages which, in places, still survive today.

CELTS
BRITAIN

CELTS

CELTS

CELTS

FRANCE
(GAUL)

CELTS

CELTS

SPAIN

ITALY

CELTS

Rome

MEDITERRANEAN SEA

A chief shows how brave he is by fighting without his helmet.

Prisoners of war are sold as slaves. Britain was a good source of slaves for the Romans.

At home

The Celts lived in thatched, wooden huts and wove wool in tartan patterns for clothes. Their craftsmen were very skilled at making wonderful objects in bronze and gold. Their bards made up great poems which they recited from memory.

Farming

The Celts in Gaul invented a reaping machine, which was copied by the Romans. They stored their grain for the winter in pits. Hunting wild boar, their favourite food, was a great sport. The children played a game rather like hockey.

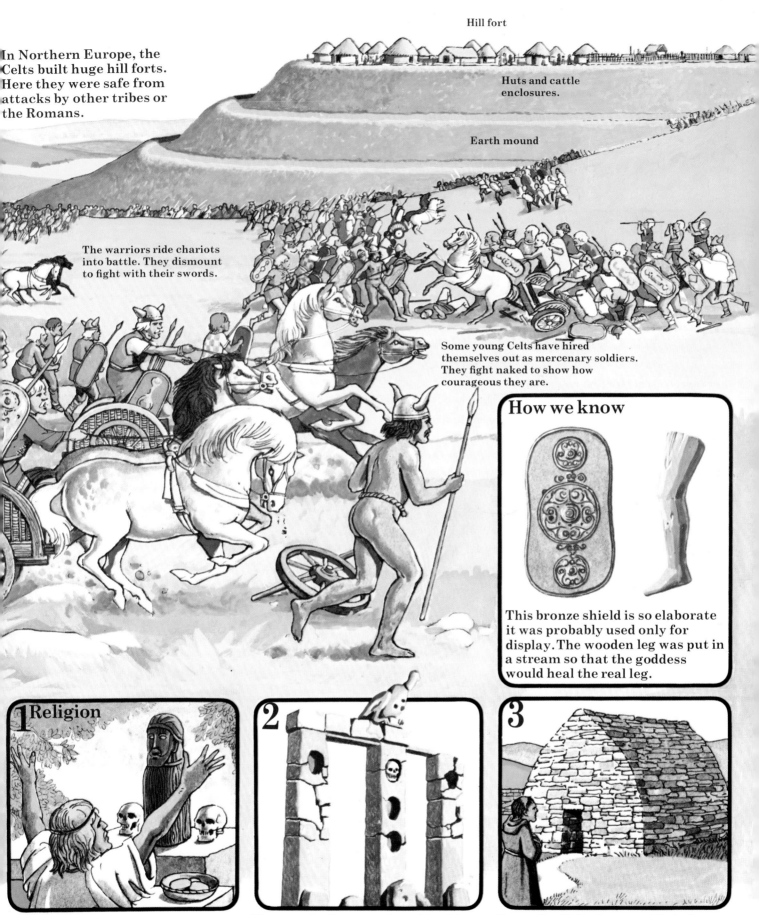

In Northern Europe, the Celts built huge hill forts. Here they were safe from attacks by other tribes or the Romans.

Hill fort

Huts and cattle enclosures.

Earth mound

The warriors ride chariots into battle. They dismount to fight with their swords.

Some young Celts have hired themselves out as mercenary soldiers. They fight naked to show how courageous they are.

How we know

This bronze shield is so elaborate it was probably used only for display. The wooden leg was put in a stream so that the goddess would heal the real leg.

1 Religion
The Celts had priests, called Druids. It took many years to become a Druid. He had to train his memory so he could learn, and hand on, the laws and customs of the tribes.

2
Human skulls were placed in this monument at Roquepertuse, France. Human remains, probably from sacrifices, have been found in pits at some religious centres of the Celts.

3
Later the Celts became Christians. They set up communities of monks in remote parts of Ireland and Scotland. Some, such as St Columba, were sent to convert the heathens.

85

The Rise of Rome

1 The city of Rome began as a small village on one of seven hills. More villages were built until they joined up into one big town.

2 At first Rome was ruled by kings, the last of whom was an Etruscan. Later, the people rebelled and set up a "republic" (a state without a king).

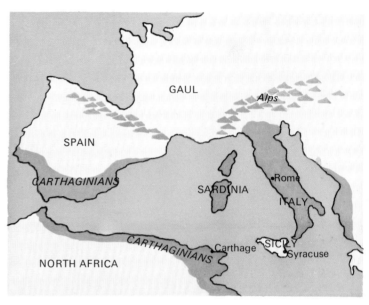

3 The Romans conquered other peoples in Italy. They fought the Carthaginians whose leader, Hannibal, invaded Italy in 218BC.

4 Men who fought for Rome settled down to farm the land they had conquered. They brought the Roman way of life to the provinces.

5 People captured in battle were made Roman slaves. One called Spartacus, who was trained as a gladiator, led a slave revolt in 71BC.

The Etruscans

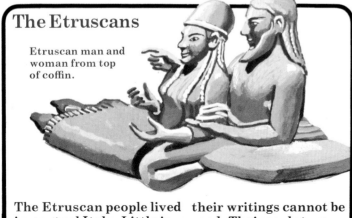

Etruscan man and woman from top of coffin.

The Etruscan people lived in central Italy. Little is known about them and their writings cannot be read. Their sculpture shows Greek influence.

Roman roads

Flat stones
Rubble
Stones
Ditch

Roman soldiers built thousands of miles of good roads. Troops could march quickly along them to control the huge empire they had captured.

The end of the Republic

1

2

3

4

In Rome many men plotted to gain control and there were civil wars. Julius Caesar, a great general, marched his army to Rome in 49BC.

Caesar soon gained power and brought peace. But one group, fearing he planned to make himself king, stabbed him to death on the Ides (the 15th) of March 44BC.

There were more civil wars until Octavian, Caesar's heir, defeated his rival, Mark Antony. Antony and his wife, Cleopatra, Queen of Egypt, killed themselves.

Octavian was given the title Augustus and later became the first emperor of Rome. He restored order in the army and revived old Roman customs.

The Roman army

The well-trained Roman armies spread outwards from Rome, gradually winning more and more territory. The soldiers laid siege to enemy forts, marching up to the walls under a roof of shields. They built wooden towers to scale the walls and broke down gates with a battering ram, roofed with skins.

When marching through enemy lands, the soldiers set up a camp each night. They rounded up animals and cut crops for food.

They used catapults to fling huge stones on to the defenders. A soldier carried the standard which was crowned by the legion's eagle.

Life in the Roman Empire

The rule of Emperor Augustus brought an end to the Roman republic with elected leaders. In its place, a peaceful empire was set up.

Inside the well-guarded Roman frontiers, new cities grew up where no towns had been before. Fine temples and houses of brick or stone were built in all parts of the empire, from Britain to North Africa. The people in the provinces traded for the goods they needed and paid government taxes for the upkeep of the army.

In the cities, fresh water was brought from the hills by aqueducts. Then it flowed along lead pipes to street fountains and houses. There were baths where people could wash and swim. Food and wine were shipped from the provinces to the city docks.

Streets were paved with stone and had drains to keep them clean.

Aqueduct

Baths

Wheat from the provinces.

Statue of emperor

Gladiator fights

People flocked to the big arenas, called amphitheatres, in the cities. There they watched fights to the death between gladiators and wild animals or condemned criminals.

Country life

Although there were many towns and cities, most people lived in the country. Rich men had large estates, looked after for them by farmers who paid them rents with money, food or animals. On the estates were grand houses, called villas, where the rich families lived with their servants and slaves. Workers on the estates grew vegetables, wheat, fruit, grapes for making wine, and olives for oil. They kept hens and geese, cows, sheep and goats. Oil and wine were stored in big pottery jars half-buried in the courtyard.

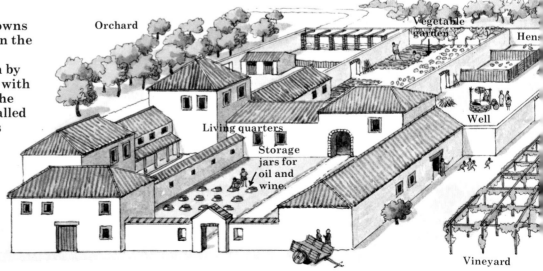

Orchard

Vegetable garden

Hens

Living quarters

Storage jars for oil and wine.

Well

Vineyard

Amphitheatre

Temple

Laws were carved on stone plaques on the walls.

Roman coins

The Romans had many different coins, made by the government. The pictures on them were often of an event or new law.

Pompeii

1

A volcano, called Mount Vesuvius, towers over the Bay of Naples in Italy. In AD79, it erupted, sending choking fumes and ashes down on the towns at its base. The city of Pompeii was buried by rivers of scorching lava.

Archaeologists have now dug through the lava and found the city. It is a record of Roman life, preserved in great detail.

2

The shape of a round loaf of bread, still on a plate, was preserved by the lava. Some people and animals choked to death in the fumes. This dog was chained up when it died.

Mosaics were used to decorate the floors of the villas. Often they show scenes from country life like this farmer digging the soil around his grape vines.

The ordinary people had very little of their own. They grew what food they could on rented land for their families and for sale. This man is driving his cow to a city market.

3

Many houses, with coloured paintings on their walls, have been found under the lava. Some paintings, like this one, were portraits of people who lived there.

Romans and Barbarians

After Augustus, the Roman empire was ruled well by strong emperors. Armies guarded its frontiers and many people became its citizens. From the time of Emperor Marcus Aurelius, however, the empire was troubled by barbarian invasions. The Roman armies grew more powerful and began to set up their own leaders as emperors, which led to civil wars. Eventually Emperor Diocletian divided the empire into four parts, each with its own capital city.

1 Hadrian's Wall

In the Roman provinces, forts protected the frontiers. Emperor Hadrian had forts, linked by a huge wall, built across northern England to keep out the barbarians.

2 Shapur / Roman emperor

Rome's old enemies, the Persians, attacked the frontiers, led by Shapur. Emperor Valerian marched against him but was defeated and captured at Edessa in AD260.

3

The emperors tried to pay for larger armies by minting extra money. Bronze coins were coated with silver to look more valuable. People needed sacks of them to pay their taxes.

4

People wanted to blame someone for the empire's troubles. They picked on the Christians who would not worship Roman gods. Thousands were killed in the arenas.

5

Tribes searching for new land invaded Northern Italy. Emperor Aurelian drove them out and had walls built round Rome as the empire's centre was no longer safe.

The Jews

Jar in which scroll was kept.

Dead Sea scroll.

Jews in Palestine rebelled against the Romans, who destroyed Jerusalem in AD70. One group lived in caves near the Dead Sea and hid their religious writings there.

The Christians

Some people in Palestine followed a religious leader called Jesus. They were known as Christians because he was called Christ, the Messiah, and met secretly in catacombs

Fish symbol for Christ

Victory over death

Chi-rho sign

The Christians used secret symbols. The fish was a symbol for Christ. The Chi-rho sign is the first two letters of Christ in Greek. The palm leaf means victory over death.

The empire splits up

Statue of the Tetrarchs which now stands in Venice.

1 Wars on several frontiers made the empire difficult to control. Emperor Diocletian divided it into four parts, each with a ruler, or "tetrarch"; two junior and two senior.

2 Diocletian's successors fought for power. Constantine beat his rival at the Milvian Bridge in Rome. He had dreamed he would win if he carried the Christian symbol.

3 Constantine then became a Christian and set up a new capital, called after him at the old Greek city of Byzantium. Later Emperor Theodosius II built walls round it.

The Barbarians

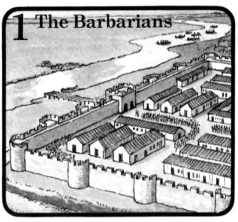

1 People in the Roman empire asked barbarians to protect them against other barbarians. But the attacks went on. In Britain, forts and look-out towers were built to guard the coasts.

Stilicho's wife / Stilicho

2 Roman emperors, in need of good soldiers, paid barbarians to lead their armies. Stilicho, a Vandal, commanded all troops and married the niece of Theodosius I.

3 The fiercest barbarians, the Huns, came from central Asia and had driven many people into Roman lands. Their leader, Attila, was called "the scourge of God".

Buried treasure

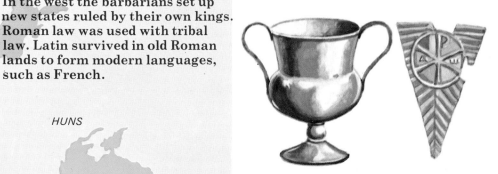

Hadrian's Wall
ANGLES
CELTS
SAXONS
JUTES
CELTS
FRANKS
HUNS
OSTROGOTHS
VISIGOTHS
ITALY
•Rome
Byzantium
(Constantinople)
VANDALS
•Carthage
MEDITERRANEAN SEA
•Jerusalem

In the west the barbarians set up new states ruled by their own kings. Roman law was used with tribal law. Latin survived in old Roman lands to form modern languages, such as French.

The Romans often buried their treasures to hide them from attacking barbarians. These Christian silver objects, which are about 1,600 years old, were dug up in a field in England.

The Byzantine Empire

The city of Constantinople resisted attacks by barbarians and became the capital of the eastern half of the Roman empire. This eastern empire lasted for more than 1,000 years and is called the Byzantine empire.

In the sixth century AD, some land captured by the barbarians was won back. The armies of Emperor Justinian regained Italy from the Ostrogoths and North Africa from the Vandals. But there were costly wars with the rival Persian empire.

The court of Justinian

Justinian's wife Theodora was a clever and powerful woman who helped rule.

The imperial guards have Christian signs on their shields.

Silk for robes worn by rich people came only from China and the Persians made trade difficult. Monks, so the story goes, brought silk worms to Justinian to start a silk industry.

Mosaics

The Romans decorated the walls and floors of their houses with small cubes of coloured stone. These are called mosaics. At the time of Justinian, coloured glass, sometimes with gold set in it, was used, and even precious stones.

How to make a mosaic

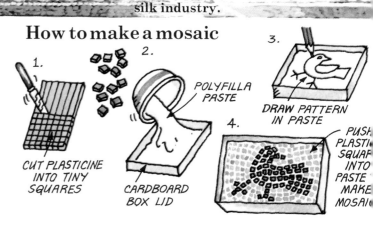

1. CUT PLASTICINE INTO TINY SQUARES
2. POLYFILLA PASTE — CARDBOARD BOX LID
3. DRAW PATTERN IN PASTE
4. PUSH PLASTIC SQUARE INTO PASTE MAKE MOSAIC

Roll out plasticine and cut it into tiny squares (1). Mix Polyfilla with water to make a thick paste and pour it into a small box lid (2). Draw a picture in the paste (3). Before the paste sets, push the coloured plasticine squares into it to make a mosaic, like this (4.

92

Chariot race

Many customs were brought from Rome. Chariot racing in the circus became mixed with politics. In a great riot, 30,000 supporters of the Blue and Green parties were killed.

The earliest Christian monks built monasteries in Egypt. Some wanted to live alone in great discomfort to prove their faith. One monk, Simon, spent years on a pillar.

In the monasteries, monks copied out manuscripts of Christian writings and older Greek works. They kept up the skills of painting ikons (images) of holy people.

Barbarian kingdoms

KINGDOM OF THE FRANKS

KINGDOM OF THE VISIGOTHS

OSTROGOTHS
ITALY
•Rome

Constantino

BYZANTINE EMPIRE
at the time of Justinian

MEDITERRANEAN SEA

King Recceswinth's crown

His name

Justinian's empire is shown here. In the west are the beginnings of several European kingdoms. The Franks have settled in France and Germany, and the Visigoths in Spain.

The Visigoths were a Germanic people. This crown was put in a church as an offering by King Recceswinth. It may have been made by Byzantine craftsmen.

The Ostrogoths settled in Italy and were finally defeated by Justinian. They made jewellery in eagle designs. The Anglo-Saxon gold cross was worn as a Christian symbol.

Key dates

753BC	Traditional date of founding of Rome.
575BC	Rome ruled by Etruscan kings.
509BC	Romans set up republic.
264/241BC	First war with Carthage.
218BC	Second war with Carthage. **Hannibal** crossed the Pyrenees.
200BC	Rome began conquest of eastern Mediterranean.
146BC	Romans destroyed Carthage and Corinth.
73/71BC	**Spartacus** led slave revolt.
58–51BC	**Julius Caesar** conquered Celts in Gaul.
44BC	**Julius Caesar** murdered in Rome.
30BC	**Antony and Cleopatra** committed suicide.
27BC	**Octavian** called Augustus; beginning of Roman Empire.
AD14	Death of **Augustus.**
AD70	Temple at Jerusalem destroyed.
AD79	Eruption of Vesuvius; Pompeii destroyed.
AD117/38	**Hadrian** was emperor; built wall across north of England.
AD161/180	**Marcus Aurelius** was emperor.
AD235	Barbarian invasions and civil wars began.
AD249/250	First persecution of Christians under Emperor **Decius**.
AD270/275	**Aurelian** was emperor; built wall round city of Rome.
AD285/305	**Diocletian** was emperor.
AD312	**Constantine** won battle of Milvian Bridge.
AD330	Dedication of city of Constantinople.
AD395	Division of Roman empire into East and West.
AD527/565	**Justinian** was emperor.

Time Chart

	Mesopotamia and Persia	**Egypt**	**Africa**	**Mediterranean lands of Europe**
	Development of farming. Rise of city-states in Sumer. Pottery being made. Cuneiform writing invented. Wheel invented.	Development of farming. Pottery being made. Hieroglyphs invented.	Rock drawings in middle of Sahara showing animals and people.	Stone monuments built, eg in Malta.
3000BC	Early Dynastic period in Sumer (First 2 dynasties of rulers). Royal graves of Ur.	Unification of Egypt. ARCHAIC PERIOD in Egypt. OLD KINGDOM. Step Pyramids built.		EARLY MINOAN PERIOD in Crete.
2500BC	**Sargon** of Akkad. The Gutians invade. Dynasty III of Ur.	Straight-sided pyramids built.		
2000BC	Arrival of the Amorites. Rise of Babylon. Reign of King **Hammurabi** of Babylon. Rise of Assyria, under King **Shamsi-Adad I.**	MIDDLE KINGDOM. Conquest of Nubia. Invasion by Hyksos.		MIDDLE MINOAN PERIOD in Crete. Picture writing (hieroglyphs) in use in Crete. Palaces built in Crete. LATE MINOAN PERIOD in Crete. Rise of Mycenaeans in Greece.
1500BC	Kassites rule Babylon.  The Mitanni rule in northern Mesopotamia. Arrival of the Persians.	NEW KINGDOM. Conquest of empire. Valley of Kings in use. Warrior pharaohs in power. **Queen Hatshepsut.** **Tutankhamun**		Eruption of Thera. Linear B writing in use in Crete. Fall of Crete, destruction of Palace of Knossos.
1000BC	Rise and fall of ASSYRIAN EMPIRE. Rise of NEW BABYLONIAN EMPIRE. Rule of **Nebuchadnezzar** in Babylon. Birth of prophet **Zarathushtra.**	LATE PERIOD Slow decline. Invasion by Assyrians and Kushites.	Beginnings of Kingdom of Kush. Spread of iron working. Carthage founded by Phoenician princess **Dido.** Capital of Kush moved to Meroe.	Decline of Mycenaeans. Arrival of Dorians in Greece. DARK AGES in Greece. Greek poet **Homer** alive. Etruscans in Northern Italy. Traditional date of founding of Rome 753BC City-states in Greece.
500BC	PERSIAN EMPIRE at its height. Conquests of **Alexander the Great** (including Persian empire).	Egyptian revival Conquest by Persia, then Alexander the Great. Rule of the Ptolemies. **Cleopatra.** Conquest by Rome.	Carthage at war with Rome (Punic wars). **Hannibal.** Carthage defeated. North Africa part of Roman empire.	Persian wars between Greeks and Persians. City of Athens very powerful. Peloponnesian War in Greece. Rule of **Pericles** in Athens. **Alexander the Great.** Rise of Rome. **Julius Caesar.** **Augustus,** Roman emperor.
0	SASSANIAN EMPIRE	Part of Roman Empire.	Meroe conquered by **King Ezana** of Axum. Slow movement of people across central and southern Africa. Arrival of barbarians (Vandals) in North Africa.	ROMAN EMPIRE. Spread of Christianity. Split of Roman empire into West and East. BYZANTINE EMPIRE. Byzantine empire ruled by Emperor **Justinian.**
AD500		Hieroglyphs fall into disuse.		